VIOLENT DELIGHTS & MIDSUMMER DREAMS

A Gothic Anthology of Shakespeare Retellings

Edited by
CASSANDRA L. THOMPSON

with
DAMON BARRET ROE

QUILL & CROW
PUBLISHING HOUSE

Violent Delights & Midsummer Dreams
Edited by Cassandra L. Thompson, Damon Barret Roe
Published by Quill & Crow Publishing House

This books contains short stories that are works of fiction. All incidents, dialogue, and characters, except for some well-known historical and public figures, are either products of the author's imagination or used in a fictitious manner. Any resemblance to actual persons, living or dead, or actual events is purely coincidental.

Copyright © 2023 by Cassandra L. Thompson. Melissa Brinks, Sabrina Howard, Erin Keating, LK Kitney, Amelia Mangan, Cedrick May, Mathew L Reyes, Emma Selle, and William Steffen.

All rights reserved. Published in the United States by Quill & Crow Publishing House, Ohio. No portion of this book may be reproduced in any form without permission from the publisher, except as permitted by U.S. copyright law.

Cover Design by Damon Barret Roe

Interior by Cassandra L. Thompson

Printed in the United States of America

ISBN (ebook): 978-1-958228-42-5

ISBN (paperback): 978-1-958228-43-2

Publisher's Website: www.quillandcrowpublishinghouse.com

"These violent delights have violent ends. And in their triumph die, like fire and powder, which as they kiss consume."

— WILLIAM SHAKESPEARE, ROMEO & JULIET

FOREWORD

Is Shakespeare Gothic?

I'll admit, my study of Shakespeare's works pales in comparison to my study of Gothic literature, so I won't pretend to be an expert here. There are scores of lovely academic journals that answer this very question. But what I can say is, as a woman who can find Gothic tropes in almost everything, it isn't hard to see them throughout Shakespeare's plays. From dramatic spectacles to eerie supernatural vibes, many of his tales evoke the same sense of dreadful suspense that would later come to define Gothic literature. In short, Hamlet is goth AF.

When the idea to do an anthology of Shakespeare retellings came about, it seemed a natural choice for a publishing house dedicated to all things odd and macabre. But like all the anthologies we've produced, there is the initial worry that writers won't be receptive. I'm happy to report, this was not the case.

Sequestered within this volume are stories bloody, dramatic, and spectacular. We hope that you will love these tales as much as we have, and perhaps discover a new favorite writer or two. It has been a pleasure to put together another Quill & Crow anthology and I hope to do

FOREWORD

so again one day. Until then, please enjoy another anthology full of dread and woe.

Dreadfully Yours,
Cassandra L. Thompson

A DOCUMENT IN MADNESS

(HAMLET)

MELISSA BRINKS

Ophelia is picking flowers.
    No, she is trying to drown herself.
    No, she is doing both.
    She perches like a thrush on a willow branch, hands outstretched, fingers reaching for one perfect blossom. A single flower won't grow over the grief chewing her from the inside; her father, yes, but also her mother, who died and left her surrounded by all these men and one distant queen. One single flower in her hair won't charm her lover back to her. She knows this and thinks she may be a fool for trying. They have called her worse. If she is beautiful, or if she is dead, perhaps they will speak more kindly of her.
    The bough breaks—you'd have to be mad to rely on the strength of a willow branch—and she falls. For one moment, the real girl's outstretched hand meets the hand of her foolish reflection, and they merge with a deafening splash. Briefly, she floats there on the surface, light and delicate as a fallen flower borne on the current.
    But her skirts drag her down, as they so often do. She struggles, reaching for the surface as the bottom of the brook calls to her, seizing her dress in icy hands. Her fingertips only just break the water. Long, loose hair tangles about her face, blinding her.

If she was trying to drown herself, she is no longer. Death stares at her from the shore, black-eyed and stern. The willow's long branches stretch above her as if to offer her a hand. She tears her expensive fabrics to break free; her dress, at last, rips and floats away, but it is too late. She breathes water and chokes, kicking her legs and flailing. She's gone too low, the dark water above her head endless and insurmountable.

She stops struggling. Her limbs, pale as the moon, relax. She floats to the surface.

When they find her later, naked, they weep. She stirs, but no one sees. Her eyelashes flutter. She isn't ready yet.

❦

Ophelia wakes, but different. She lays atop a stone slab, arms crossed over her chest. They've put her in a shroud, a ghastly, gauzy thing that hides her body from the world. She shreds it between her fingernails and, stretching death's ache from her joints, she rises. She plucks buds from her funeral flowers and weaves them into her hair.

She is aware that Death took her hand and escorted her elsewhere. Perhaps Death brought her back, too; nobody wants a mad girl. Being both dead *and* mad, she no longer has anything to fear—not the stares of the royal family, not the judgment of her brother, not the scorn of her lover. There were words she couldn't say before she died. Punishments to be dealt out. It all seems so much easier now.

A smile tugs at her lips. Someone will open the door to her tomb soon enough.

❦

Daylight streams through the crack in the door and she covers her eyes with the back of her hand. It stings, but her eyes grow accustomed to the light; it takes longer to adjust to the screams and cries that greet her. The tomb is quiet, and the rush of people is anything but.

Ophelia, skin pink and heart beating once again, is ushered at once into her brother's arms. Allowing him to hug her, she smiles. But she slips from his grasp, running barefoot to the hole in the ground meant to hold her body. What a lovely group has gathered for what ought to have been her funeral. Her brother, the Queen, the King. Her father is absent, his mouth full of dirt. Her lover, here, looking surprised, disheveled, out of sorts. He—clad all in black, a sorry but familiar sight—does not look at her.

Ophelia notes the knot between his brows, the way his fingers tense into a fist. He knows something she doesn't. He knows *many* things she doesn't, and she wants to pluck those things like pearls from his mouth and braid them into her hair.

She doesn't speak, but she hums, a wild, merry tune soon stuck in the heads of all who hear it. Her brother begs her to stop, lest they think her mad. She pauses, smiles, and begins anew. They already thought her mad. Now they will know it.

༺༻

Her lover watches her, stroking his chin. He does not speak to her. He does not speak to many, not since he returned from his aborted journey to England. There are secrets in his mouth, behind his teeth, beneath his tongue. To open his mouth is to let them spill out. His jaw is tense with the effort of keeping them all in.

She plants a merry kiss upon his cheek.

He doesn't move, but his whole body stiffens.

She smiles, leans in closer, and seizes his earlobe between her teeth. "*I know you*," she whispers, and a shiver runs through him.

She leaves him, but not without a glance backward to watch his throat bob with a hard swallow. What secrets has he choked down?

༺༻

Her lover cannot take his eyes off of her after that. Sometimes they are narrowed, sometimes wide; moods flick over his face faster than she can name them. She carries on humming, dancing barefoot through the halls, her elegant limbs outstretched as if she were about to tumble from a willow branch.

He has had enough. He presses her to the wall, his forearm to her chest, fury in his eyes and liquor on his breath. "You drowned," he said. "They found your body. I didn't see it—"

"I see yours," she says, laughing. "I see you now, dark and stormy and"—she gasps, raising her eyebrows—"mad." Ophelia presses a finger to his chest, drags it down, down, down, loops it through the waist of his trousers. "I see you, mad boy."

"How did you do it?" he asks. There's sick hope in his voice.

"How indeed." She cocks her head and a curl falls into her face. A crown of flowers rests atop her head—rue, of course, and violets, purple little bells all woven in her tangles.

Her lover seizes her by the wrist, encircling it all the way round.

She lifts her chin to meet his eyes. There's fear there, and her lips twitch. She blinks, the flutter of her eyelashes as delicate as a butterfly's slow basking.

"Tell me, Ophelia," he says. It's a rare thing to hear her name—most people reserve it for the woman who died, not the woman who came back. "Tell me what happened."

"You are what you pretend to be," she says, her words a little song. "We're all just players. You most of all."

Her lover tenses, slams his fist into the wall, but she doesn't move. "What game are you playing?"

Unhooking her finger from his trousers, she slips away from him. "None at all."

❦

Her brother insists she wash her feet, crusted with dirt as they are. She refuses, won't even let warm water touch her. A doctor is called, pronounces her mad, but everyone knows that already, especially her lover who watches her through narrowed eyes. He envies her for the attention. No one notices his antics when Ophelia's dancing through the halls laughing, singing songs in languages no one has ever heard.

Her brother casts long, angry looks at her lover, and she smiles. How lovely it is to be wanted, to be seen and heard and fussed over.

How lovely it is to be not worth disguising your hateful glares or hushing your voice for.

These looks and words are useful secrets. She ties knots in her hair to remember them by.

✥

"Leave me, please," her lover pleads with her.

She follows him from room to room as he paces, tugging at his hair as he thinks aloud.

"Lord, shall I lie in your lap?" she asks, and sticks her tongue out between her lips.

"Ophelia," he says.

"Yes, Lord?"

"Leave me."

She does not. She shuffles after him, mimicking; she tugs at her own hair, whispers, jabs her finger into her palm, until he turns and grabs her by the wrist.

"What are you? Another ghost?"

"Another, Lord? Who else haunts you?"

"So you *are* a ghost?"

Ophelia laughs and cups him through his trousers. "A ghost with such appetites! I think not."

Her lover makes a pained sound and lets go of her wrist, stepping away. "Another thing sent to torture me."

She laughs and encircles his waist with her thin arms. "Only if you wish."

"I am tortured enough," he says. He shrugs off her embrace, taking long strides away from her.

She follows as dutifully as a shadow. "By whom, Lord? Should I be jealous?"

Her lover shoots her a venomous look. Expressions move across his face like clouds over water, until his shoulders relax and he collapses into a plush chair. "My father."

She sits before him, cross-legged. "Your father is dead."

"So were you."

She smiles.

"His ghost speaks to me. It says my uncle murdered him, poured poison in his ear. It asks me to avenge him."

"And have you?"

"My uncle still lives, still beds my mother, still wears my father's crown."

Ophelia leans forward, wiggling her body until she is laying on her chest with her feet in the air. "Will you kill him?"

He is silent and still while she kicks her feet back and forth, slow and leisurely, as if she were out for a pleasant swim.

"I must."

"How will you do it?"

He pulls at his hair again, suddenly anxious. "I don't *know*. He's proven his guilt to me—"

"How?"

"The play," he says. "It was a re-enactment of what the ghost told me of my father's death."

"Ha!" she says, and rolls onto her back. "Clever boy. You laid a trap and he stepped into it."

"Precisely. But—"

"How will you do the deed? A sword through the chest, just like my dear father?" She mimes a thrust, twists her wrist to drive it home. Upside-down, she sees his features darken.

"It was an accident."

"Oh, yes," she says, nodding so fast, the room turns to a blur. "You stretched out your hand and Death met your fingertips."

"I didn't mean to do it, Ophelia. I thought he was my uncle, that I'd be done with the whole bloody affair right then. And my behavior afterward..." He pauses.

She imagines she can see inside his mind, the way he gropes for words that will appease her.

"I had to act mad. Everything I did was a means to convince my uncle I wasn't worth being suspicious of. I had no reason to kill your father."

"You were *acting*, Lord?"

"Only acting, yes," he says with a sigh. "He had no qualms about

A DOCUMENT IN MADNESS

killing my father. If he knew I knew, he'd kill me too, and I cannot rest until justice is done."

She rolls back onto her stomach, her chin in her hands. "How do you act mad?"

Her lover's mouth opens, shuts again. "Unpredictable," he says. "Nonsensical. I speak in ways where they can't grasp my meaning."

She sits up then, crawls forward, and drapes herself across his lap.

He squirms, but he can't move her without shoving her off, and despite the madness, he does not.

Ophelia looks up at him, batting her long eyelashes slowly, as if she were underwater. "Like me."

A pause stretches between them, long and thin as a strand of spider's silk. Her lover doesn't speak, so she raises both her hands, fingers pinched to her thumbs.

With one, in a deep voice, she says, "Ophelia, darling, dearest, I acted mad *before* you went mad." With the other, in a voice higher-pitched than her own, she replies, "You speak as if the two things can be separated!"

"Hm," says the first voice, and points its beaked face toward the ground in thought.

"All your unkindness—" says puppet Ophelia, voice shaky with an actor's practiced tremor.

"False!" says the first voice. "Faked! Of course I care for you, dearest girl, but I *must* spurn you, I *must* murder your father, because my father's ghost spoke to me!"

The puppet with the high voice fixes the deep-voiced puppet with a stare. "So you *are* mad."

"No, darling, no—it's faked, to throw my enemies off the scent!" The deep-voiced puppet speaks with a note of hysteria.

"If one feels compelled to act mad," says puppet Ophelia, "and one indulges the impulse, is that not the same thing as being mad?"

Her lover—the real one—pushes Ophelia's hands down and away, ending the show. "Please," he says, his voice pained. "I can't bear this."

"Oh?" she asks. Her hands relax, creeping through her lover's hair.

He stiffens, but does not pull away.

"What will happen if you can't bear it? Will you go mad?"

"Ophelia," he says, his voice a warning.

She may be mad, but she is not stupid. She slips off his lap and lets her feet carry her out of the room and away.

The conversation, the longest she's had since she came back, seems to have sapped the life from her. She spends more hours outdoors despite the growing chill in the air. The blossoms have died, but she crushes their yellowed petals in her fist anyway. They smell of dust and the thick, sweet odor of decay. The brook is even colder now than when it took her, but still she dips her toes in. They turn red, then blue, until her brother grabs her under her arms and drags her away, chastising her for getting too close to the thing that nearly killed her.

"Nearly," she repeats, sleepy with the effort. But with the cold nipping at her feet, she feels strength return to her body. She must rest. There is work to be done.

Her brother has one eye on her, always, to catch her misbehaving. He was never this protective before she died; she supposes it's his way of clinging to the last thing he has that still breathes.

"*You're* alive," she says, as he drags her back to the chamber that used to be hers.

"Yes, and so are you. You'll die if you catch cold."

"I *did* die, though."

"You didn't. You nearly died."

"I came back."

He stops, and spins her to face him. "You can't say that. That's blasphemy."

"I thought one must always tell the truth."

Her brother's mouth opens and closes like a fish.

She moves to touch his chin, to help him speak, but he moves out of the way.

"Just stop, please."

"You think I don't know what the truth is." It isn't a question. "But I do."

He regards her with curiosity. "You're calm today."

She makes an exaggerated show of yawning. "I'm tired. My bed is too warm. I want to see the stars."

"No."

"Are you mad, brother?"

He sighs, shedding the breath like a heavy thing. "No. I'm only worried about you." His voice trembles like a leaf in a breeze. "You're all I have left. It scares me that you keep coming so close to the thing that almost took you away from me."

"No, brother. Are you *mad?*" She stretches the word out until it's several syllables long, punctuating the question by sticking her tongue out.

"What? No, I'm not—"

"I heard you planned to kill the prince." Ophelia doesn't say where she heard this. She isn't certain, herself; perhaps it was a whisper in the hall, or an overheard conversation, or perhaps the brook told her. But she knows he thinks her lover's death would be not only necessary, but good. As if Denmark isn't awash in enough blood to stain the soil red for generations. As if the Queen's chambers don't sometimes have the stink of death about them.

Her brother flushes, and mutters to himself. "Don't be ridiculous. That's regicide, or near enough. Don't say things like that."

"I think one must be a little mad to kill someone, don't you?"

"People kill one another all the time in war. Are all soldiers mad?" Her brother hauls her toward her chambers with renewed vigor.

She lets him drag her along, considering his words. "Yes," she says. "We make them that way."

He stops again and turns to face her. "You mustn't talk like this. Do you know what they do with women who...who say such things? They send them away, or lock them up, and they're never heard from again."

"That's what you thought happened to me. You thought you'd never hear my voice again, that I'd slipped somewhere out of your reach." As if to illustrate, she dances away from him, her freed hand running along the wall. She is only teasing; she runs toward her chambers, laughing as he follows. She stops, suddenly, before her door frame—the door has been removed so she can be watched at any moment—and he nearly crashes into her. "Would you send me to such a fate yourself?"

Her brother takes a moment to catch his breath. "I don't *want* to. But I can't control what other people do with you." His words fade to silence, but there's something hanging in the air, unspoken.

Sister, she thinks. *He used to call me sister.*

"And what do you think?" she asks. Her fingers trace the woodwork on her door frame. "Do you think it would be better if I were elsewhere, silent?"

"No, of course not," he says, words jostling one another to make it out of his mouth first.

Ophelia presses a finger lightly to his nose. "Then be careful what you call me." She turns and strides to her bed, where she sleeps soundly and dreams of nothing.

❦

Her lover calls her to his chambers. She goes, light-footed. Ophelia has dipped her feet into the brook enough that they are pink and clean again, though her hair is a nest of wild curls and flowers and knots, one for each secret.

He awaits her, looking troubled and dark as a storm cloud. His chin to his fist, he is deep in thought—he doesn't seem to notice she's arrived, despite summoning her himself, until she presses a light kiss to his cheek and laughs when he is startled. Her lover is slow to come out of his thoughts, shaking the quiet like a great beast shaking off dirt after a long slumber.

"I owe you an apology, Ophelia."

She lets the silence linger between them, delighting in how he speaks her name like a precious thing. There are fairy tales about people who make wishes and horrible things tumble from their mouths—toads, gemstones, poison—but the way he speaks her name is musical, a gift. She sometimes forgets what it is now that only he will speak it aloud. "Ophelia"—from the Greek for "helper"—what a blessing it is to be called by her role. Or perhaps what *was* her role. Now she thinks of herself less as helper and more as burr.

Finally, satisfied with the way he shifts in discomfort, she says, "An apology? For what, my Lord?"

"I was unkind to you. Cruel. And then—your father—"

"As you said, an accident."

"It was, I swear it. But I viewed him as collateral damage, and I ought to have been viewing him as your father." He pauses, and his throat bobs with a harsh swallow.

She thinks about sinking her teeth into it, biting the apple fabled to be hiding there beneath his skin—a new forbidden fruit.

"As my beloved's father."

She smiles at that. Before she drowned, she looked away when she smiled, as if showing too much joy was shameful. Now, she smiles with teeth.

"I beg your forgiveness, Ophelia. I am not owed it, but only you and Horatio know the truth. I need allies, or at the very least, I need to preserve my relationships with people I trust. And people I trust are in short supply. I understand if you cannot forgive me, but you must understand that no matter the anger I may have felt toward your father, I would never have taken his life intentionally." Suddenly, he clasps her hands. Though people have touched her since she returned, rarely has it been with tenderness. "Whatever you ask in atonement, I will give it."

He moves from the chair and kneels before her, his hands gently holding hers. He kisses her knuckles, then looks up at her face. Tears glisten in the corners of his eyes.

She smiles again, with teeth. "Only a kiss, my Lord."

"A kiss."

"A kiss," she says, and leans forward.

He rises, and cups her face in his hands. His lips are soft on hers.

She bites his lip hard enough to split it. Her lover cries out and presses the back of his hand to his mouth, anger and fear flashing in his eyes. A prince is used to taking, not to having things taken from him.

She laughs and licks a drop of blood from her own lip. Then

Ophelia dances from the room, savoring the salty flavor left on her mouth.

Her lover keeps his distance after that. He doesn't call for her, doesn't glance at her when they're in the same room. She's taken what she needs, and she no longer feels the burning in the pit of her being when she looks at him. Instead, there's warmth. She remembers this soaring sensation in her chest from before she went into the brook. She remembers, too, the clench in her gut when he began dressing in black and speaking in nonsense. Her heart ached for him, then. Perhaps it does now, too. When she sees him, she no longer wants to torment him—no more torment than he asks for—and instead, she longs for something she can't name. She knows what it would feel like. Warmth, strength. She wraps her arms around herself as she looks at him, running fingers over gooseflesh, but he does not return her gaze.

Ophelia has learned something since she went into the brook: she likes to act, to decide. This new Ophelia would know whether she was picking flowers or drowning herself. And this Ophelia knows that she is hungry, though for what, she is unsure.

So she does not wait for her lover to summon her again. She suspects he won't; she has taken something from him he cannot get back. It's what she was owed. Blood for blood. Now they are even. The prince and the madwoman—a title for a fairy tale.

She waits for him in his chambers, sprawled across his bed like before, when her cheeks were flushed pink with embarrassment and she tried to cover her body. Those things don't worry her anymore. She lets her dress fall where it likes. How her brother would disapprove. How her father would disapprove, if she had a father. All she has is blood in her stomach and fresh dirt between her toes.

Her lover does not seem surprised to see her. His shoulders slump, his breath huffs out in a sigh. "I am tired, Ophelia," he says. "Leave me."

She does not. She props herself up on her elbow and flutters her eyelashes at him. "I miss you," she says.

A DOCUMENT IN MADNESS

He laughs, a bitter, ugly thing. "You don't."

Ophelia pours herself out of bed, letting gravity drag her to the floor legs first. Her dress hitches up around her thighs and she does not move it, only wraps her arms around her knees and sets her chin on top to watch her lover through lowered lashes. "I do. I miss you terribly."

"Terribly," he says, and touches a finger to the scab on his lip, red with fresh blood—he's been worrying at it like a beast anxiously gnawing a bone.

"Terribly," she repeats.

"What do you want, Ophelia?" His voice is heavy, like the burden he's been carrying.

"Must I want something to be here?"

He slumps into his chair, legs splayed, hand over his face. "Everybody wants something, and I have no more to give. I have one mission and I'm failing. I don't think I'll survive this. Your brother wants me dead. My uncle wants me dead. Who knows who else would have my head?"

"I would, my Lord." Ophelia leans back against the bed, letting her legs fall to each side. The stone floor is cool against her thighs. She shivers and smiles, a toothy, toothsome thing.

Her lover's breath hisses through his teeth, bringing snakes to her mind. "I know," he says, and the words come tumbling from his mouth like water, "I know, I know, I *know*. God, but I know. And you have every right! I *was* cruel to you, and your father's blood is on my hands, and now here you are—"

"What, Lord?"

He doesn't answer. Doesn't even look at her. His head is in his hands, and there's a little gasp of breath that tells her he may be crying. Ophelia only sits there smiling, scratching at the stone floor with a fingernail. She draws flowers into the grime, and lets whatever he's going through pass. In time, his breathing slows, evens, and becomes quiet; he's asleep, or near enough. She tiptoes over to him and curls up at his feet like a cat. Her lover stirs and his hand falls from his face.

"What will you do now?" she asks, her voice softer than it's been since she came back from the brook.

"I don't know," he says. There's an honesty in it, sweet as spring, that she's missed.

"Do you hate me?"

"No. I don't hate you." The edge is back, and she notes it with a knot in her hair.

"Why do you hate me?"

"As I said, I don't—"

"I don't mind if you hate me. I hate you sometimes. You killed the man I loved most."

"I don't hate you, and it was an accident, Ophelia—"

"Not him," she says. Her hand creeps up his trouser leg, fingers stroking his hair the wrong direction. "The other one."

"Who?"

Ophelia smiles, giving a cheeky pinch to his inner thigh. "My lover."

The look of concern on his face darkens. "Ophelia," he says slowly, his tongue dragging over each vowel. "Who do you think I am?"

She laughs, because it is obvious. "My lover," she says. Her lover, the Prince of Denmark, madman, fool.

He looks at her through squinted eyes, which rake over her like fingernails, scrutinizing her face as if it holds an answer. She leans in to meet his gaze, daring him to ask the question she knows haunts him.

"What do you mean?"

"You killed my lover," she says. She moves to her knees, in a supplicant's position but with one hand on each of his thighs. "You, my lover, killed you, my lover. You were so tender once. And to punish me, you—"

"No, not you, Ophelia. You did nothing wrong."

"Yet you punish me, spurn me, humiliate me—"

"Only because—"

"Because what?" She moves to his lap now, straddling him. "Because you were pretending to be mad?"

"Yes."

"Like your play. Pretending."

She can feel his breath quicken. "Yes."

"Pretending, to reveal the truth."

A DOCUMENT IN MADNESS

Silence.

She plants a soft kiss to his forehead, to his nose, to his bloodied lips. "You killed him, but death is nothing. You can bring him back, as I came back."

"I'm not *dead*, Ophelia," he says, and there's a bitterness to his words that warns of poison. "Just because I've acted poorly doesn't mean I really believe it—"

"How am I to know what you mean or don't mean?"

He stiffens, and she feels the muscles in his thighs flex. "That's funny, coming from you," he says. "You've spoken in nothing but riddles since you...since you returned."

"I have spoken truly. Have you?"

"Of course not."

"Of course not," she repeats. She climbs off of him, dusts her hands off, and places them on her waist as if she is a maid ready to scold him for nicking pastries from the kitchens. "Do you understand?"

"No, not at all."

"I loved him," she says. "I did love him, even though I was told not to. I loved him and you took him from me and you sit there now in his place, telling me nothing is wrong. There is so much blood on your hands, Lord. I don't think you can ever get them clean."

Her lover draws in a breath. She watches his chest rise, his eyes close, his nostrils flare as he lets it out slowly.

"I don't think I can get them clean, either."

"Not if you keep blaming madness." She turns, and moves to the door. She feels tired again, like her bones are weary, and thinks it is dark enough that she might make it to the brook before her brother sees her leave. "I miss my lover, and I will miss you too."

He watches her go.

She can feel his eyes on her back, on the sway of her hips, and she wishes, despite everything, that it was his bloody hands instead.

❦

There are events that Ophelia has foreseen. Now that she has spoken her piece, she does what she can to warn them, but nobody listens to a madwoman. She carves CASSANDRA into the door of her lover's chamber and her brother asks the kitchen in harsh whispers how she got her hands on a knife.

To her brother, she says she loves the Prince and she cannot stand to have another beloved thing taken away from her. He insists he would never.

She tells the Queen to drink only from her own cup, but she only returns a weak smile. To the King, she says nothing. He does not deserve her warnings.

To her lover, she brings flowers. Chamomile. Hellebore. Peony. The time for fresh flowers is past; she brings him dried petals and stems and leaves them outside his door, on his pillow, and strewn about his bath. He sends her away if she comes.

She hopes he will remember what she means. She isn't certain, so she leaves him more hints: a knife, apple seeds, a series of slashes in his favorite shirt. She feels time accelerate around her, like when she and her brother used to sled down the hills near the palace. Everything becomes a blur, a confusing smear of color and meaning, like standing too close to a painting.

And suddenly, she is in the grand hall, and her lover and her brother have swords in their hands, and the Queen is raising a toast. Ophelia cannot speak, only clench the dirty fabric of her dress into her fists and watch as everything she has seen comes to pass. She tried to warn them. She tried to get through to her lover, to her brother, to the Queen—all of them caught in various schemes and madnesses, and all unwilling to see them. She wants to scream, but she bites her tongue until she tastes blood. This will all be over soon.

The Queen dies first, the foam at her lips tinged wine-purple. The King tries to stop her, but he isn't quick enough. And then things begin in earnest; the Queen's death is the first snowflake of winter, and everything else is the storm.

Her brother cuts her lover and the poison begins its deadly work. Her lover's limbs begin to twitch, his reflexes to slow. Still, he is able to take the poisoned sword and inflict the same curse on her brother. In some far-off day, someone might consider this poetic. Ophelia can only think of Death, huge and hulking in the corner of the room,

A DOCUMENT IN MADNESS

unlikely to be moved by pretty words and this pale imitation of justice.

Her brother dies next, truth spilling from his mouth with spit and blood. There is no more room for knots in her hair. The conspiracy is revealed. Death begins to salivate.

And there is her lover, vengeance like flame in his eyes. She feels blood begin to trickle from her own mouth. Has she bitten through her tongue? She might as well, for all anyone has listened to her.

He rushes toward the King and then the King is dead on the floor, run through with the poisoned sword. Ophelia will not mourn him.

Her lover has little time for her. This is nothing new, even as he is dying. The king of Norway is coming. Her lover's friend, the observer, demands his attention. He swears he'll die at his prince's side, but her lover tells him no, he must live and tell the story, as if there is nobody else who can be trusted with it.

Ophelia squats beside her lover, his cheeks pale, spittle dribbling from his lip. His eyes are unfocused; perhaps he is looking at Death over her shoulder. She feels its cold breath.

She looks at her lover, her head cocked like a bird's.

He licks his lips, and draws a shuddering breath. "I am sorry," he says.

"I know."

"I understand what you mean, now. I did kill him. The man you loved."

"I came back," she says, touching a finger to his nose. From her sleeve, she draws a sprig of rosemary and presses it to his hand. "Take it with you."

The light flees his eyes. A cold wind brushes past her. Her lover, the man she loved; both are gone now, and what lies before her is an empty shell.

Her lover bade the king of Norway take his lands, but she has other ideas. Quick as a magpie, she sweeps the crown from the fallen king's temples and places it upon her own head. It's an ugly, heavy thing, but so is a shroud, and she wore that just fine. While the observer prepares for war or surrender or some other thing she can't name, she takes a seat on the throne. Why not? Nobody thinks to stop her. Nobody minds her, not anymore. The last people to care about her are still bleeding into the flagstones. To the rest, what is a mad girl but a buzzing fly? Easily ignored, and easily swatted. If they think her a true threat, they will strike her down.

She watches the Norwegian king enter the hall. He surveys the bodies of the royal family, the way the members of the court tense, uncertain what to do. Transferring the crown to him would betray their loyalty; and besides, there she sits with it upon her head. They might overpower her to take it, but why risk the bite?

"Who is she?" he asks, and though the court looks in her direction, nobody speaks. They haven't spoken her name since she returned from the brook. They're no longer certain that it even *is* her, especially now, crowned and seated on the throne of Denmark.

Ophelia only smiles.

The observer speaks, outlining the sorry tale, its themes and peaks and valleys, with little mention of her, and never by name—she, the cast-off lover, the mad one, the dead girl, merits only passing reference.

She isn't a fool. The crown is temporary, as it was for the King, and her lover's father before him. But while the men discuss other men, she sits atop the throne and dares them to take it from her. She is quick and mad and mourning, and she will go down with blood in her teeth or not at all.

OTHELLO—AN AMERICAN TRAGEDY

CEDRICK MAY

ACT I

BRABANZIO PLANTATION, BELL COUNTY, TEXAS, 1856– NIGHT

Emilia held a small cotton handkerchief over her nose as she eased the lantern through the barn door. She peeked in to find no one except for the several horses breathing heavily in their sleep as they stood in locked stalls. Emilia stepped into the barn, holding up her skirt to prevent it from dragging over the dirt and damp straw lining the wide central aisle between the stalls. She stopped in front of the first stall, where a waking Andalusian considered her with a large, groggy eye. The dark bay horse huffed a deep snort as it nodded at her over the stable door.

Emilia set her lantern on a large barrel nearby. The pungent smells in the barn made her eyes water as she took the handkerchief from her nose and tucked it away beneath her lace sleeve. She looked the horse in its drowsy eye.

"Why must you and I bear the weight of the world at the whim of insufferable masters?" she whispered as she stroked the horse's muzzle.

In the hard brightness of the lantern's light, Emilia considered the brown skin of her hand as it slid against the dark-bay coat of the Andalusian's neck.

The horse gave another lazy snort and tapped the floor with its foreleg. Emilia smiled at the master's prize horse, shushing it as she held its muzzle in her palms. "Quiet, sweet creature—there are secret things yet to do this night." Her smile evaporated. She reached under the folds of her thin wool cape and produced a long, crescent-shaped hand scythe, its blade glinting in the lantern light.

The horse let out a low groan.

"I wish it were different, too."

A slide latch banged against wood and Emilia jumped. She grabbed her lantern and held it aloft, gripping the scythe low at her waist in the other hand. "Who's that?" she called.

"Don't you know your husband?"

Emilia relaxed at the sound of the familiar voice. A dark, broad-shouldered man walked into the lantern light, a head taller than Emilia.

Iago still wore his soiled, sweaty clothes from his day working the fields. He took the lantern from Emilia and placed it back on the barrel before putting his hands on her shoulders. "I'd give you a hug, but I know Miss Desdemona don't like my smell on you 'fore you have to tend to her."

Emilia hugged Iago, pressing her face to his chest. "That doesn't matter tonight."

"This ain't our night to be together—you'll get in trouble if she calls and you're not there."

"There's plenty of trouble to go 'round tonight, you can be sure."

"What are you doing out here in this barn?" Iago asked. "You're out of place here away from the house. You get lost coming out to my quarters?"

"No more lost than I've ever been."

"What's this?" Iago took the scythe from Emilia's hand and inspected it. "Where'd you get this?"

Emilia hesitated, then took the scythe back from her husband. "It belongs to Othello."

"Othello?"

"It belonged to his father 'fore they took him away all those years ago. I kept it. I came tonight to give it back to him—"

"Othello!" Iago spat the name as if it were a foul taste in his mouth. "You come here to see him in secret!"

"No, I—"

"There's nothing I've ever desired that Othello couldn't wrench from me!"

"No, it's not like that!"

Iago took an angry step toward Emilia, "What's it like, then? *What's it like?* Haven't I been a good husband?" he said, beating a fist to his chest. "I know I stink of the fields, so I can't touch you else my stench will soak into your fine dresses! *My* sweat would offend the masters when you pour them the afternoon tea! And yet, *am I not loyal?* I only see you once a week because I'm too coarse in mind and manners to work in the master's house—and yet, *am I not loyal?*"

"I *am* yours," Emilia pleaded, raising her arms, "I *am* constant."

Iago pointed a finger into the darkness. "And haven't I stayed loyal to Marse Brabanzio and his family, even when they passed me over as overseer, to give that station to Othello? Othello! It was *my* family that built the house they live in, *my* family! Othello's father was an arrogant and disobedient—"

"Do not speak such gossip, husband," Emilia interjected, "we don't know—"

"*My* family has bled on this land for three generations, but it's Othello who reaps all the rewards." Iago pointed at the scythe in his wife's hand, his anger turning to tears. "Take up your blade, Emilia," he said, falling to his knees, head bowed low. "Cut me down in the name of everyone's prince, Othello!"

There was a long moment of silence amid only the sighs of horses.

Emilia tossed the scythe to the hay-covered floor. It landed in front of her kneeling husband with a dull thud. "If you wish to die," she said, "be a man and cut your own throat. Otherwise, stand up."

Iago gaped at the blade lying in the hay. He grasped the old tool by the wooden handle and rose. He held the instrument cradled in his open palms, squinting at crude markings etched deep into the sweat-stained handle.

"What are these marks? They mean something?"

"I don't know," Emilia said, "I can't read them." Iago returned the scythe to her. She placed it on the barrel next to the lantern, then turned and embraced her husband.

"I know you two used to be close," Iago said.

"We were children back then."

"My jealousy unmans me."

"I came here to talk about what he did to Uncle Saul today," Emilia said. "It's not a conversation I look forward to."

Iago looked at the Andalusian, nodding. "Your uncle didn't deserve a beating like that," he said over his shoulder. "But how did you know Othello would be here tonight?"

"The three candles in my mistress's window."

Iago looked at his wife with bewilderment. "So, they have a secret signal?"

Emilia nodded.

"Three candles..." Iago said, amused. "So, the young black ram is tupping the master's white ewe!"

"Iago! Don't say such things!"

Iago chuckled. "I should go. He's overseeing late work in the west field tonight, but he won't be far behind me."

He kissed Emilia, then went to the barn door and eased it open until there was enough room to squeeze through.

"Wait," Emilia called. She went to her husband and pulled off one of her lace sleeves, a hand-sewn *engageante* handed down to her by her mistress. "I will see you soon, love."

Iago raised the lace sleeve to his nose and smiled. "Looks like I'm a man of good fortune, after all." He disappeared into the darkness, leaving his wife alone.

Emilia returned to the barrel holding the lantern and picked up the scythe. She turned it in the light, trying to make sense of the strange etchings in its handle.

ACT II

The barn door creaked open to admit Othello's tall, powerful frame. He held a small lantern low in one hand, squinting into the bright glare of Emilia's own light. "Desdemona? You should put that out before someone sees—"

"It's me, Othello. Emilia."

Othello started at the sound of Emilia's familiar voice. He spun around to pull the barn door shut, then locked its inner latch. "Emilia! I couldn't recognize you," he said, approaching with long strides.. "Your light blinded me..." Othello hung his lantern from a hook high on a rafter. He took Emilia gently by the forearm, raising it between them into the light, caressing the fabric of her delicate floral sleeve. "I've seen this dress before—from afar. Miss Desdemona wore it once while entertaining guests on the veranda."

Emilia eased her arm from Othello's hands. "Yes. Miss Desdemona gives me her old dresses when she's finished with them. I've had this one a while."

"I haven't seen *you* for a while," Othello said. There was a silence between them as he scanned the dark regions of the barn, as if looking for someone. "What are you doing here? You always hated this place."

"I came to see you."

"How did you know I'd be here tonight?" he asked with a sideward glance.

"After what you did to Uncle Saul today, I knew *someone* had to come tend these animals."

Othello turned away. "That was necessary."

"You had him beat so bad he can't walk! All over these *damned* horses—"

"These are Master Brabanzio's horses," Othello shouted. He pointed at the Andalusian. "And *that* is his prize riding horse. Your uncle neglected his duties, and when the master came out to ride this morning, he found a split in Jerusalem's hoof—"

"My uncle's been ill," Emilia shouted back, eyes watering, "he's getting old—"

"That does not matter—"

"*Not matter?*" Emilia wiped at the tears sliding down her cheeks.

"He's my uncle! Remember when he used to swing you by your arms until you couldn't stop laughing? He taught you how to ride—"

"I had to do my job—"

"You monster! You've forgotten who you are, and they've made you into a monster!"

Othello's face went from anger to shock, and then to...something else. A something else Emilia hadn't seen in a very long time. He sat down hard on a hay bale next to the barrel with the lantern, his head in his hands. "I have lost you again."

In the quiet that fell between them, Emilia caught her breath as she wiped at the tears. She put her hand on Othello's head, rubbed her palm over his soft, curled hair. Emilia slid her hand down to his cheek and felt the day-old roughness on it. She grabbed the scythe from the barrel.

"Othello..." It was just a whisper.

Othello looked up, Emilia's hand on his cheek. She showed him the scythe, turning the implement from side to side in the lantern light. "You brought that for me?"

Emilia nodded. She took a step back, then held the scythe out to him in both hands.

He took the tool and looked it over. He stopped at the etching on the handle, staring and rubbing his fingers over the deep indentations. "Where did you find this?"

"Your father dropped it in the fields the day they came and took him away. I took it and hid it."

"That was a long time ago. How old were we? Eleven? Twelve?"

"We were ten, Othello."

Emilia cupped her hand under Othello's and raised the scythe closer to the light. She pointed at the inscription. "Is this writing? Doesn't look like anything I know."

Othello looked surprised. "You can read?"

"And write some, too."

"How's that? Marse doesn't like slaves to read."

"Miss Desdemona insisted," Emilia said. "Told Marse Brabanzio she didn't want a handmaid that couldn't help her with her letter writing."

"Still full of surprises," Othello said, smiling.

Emilia smiled back, then pointed at the handle again. "What's it say?"

Othello inspected the inscription. *"There is no god but Allah,"* he intoned.

"What's that mean?" Emilia asked, staring closer at the strange script.

"I'm not sure," Othello said. "My father taught me to write this, and a lot of other things when I was a child. This here's Islamic writing. My father was a Muslim prince before they put him on a ship and brought him here."

"So, the old rumors are true?"

Othello nodded. "They put him on one of those illegal slave ships, sold him off in Louisiana to Old Master, Marse Brabanzio's father. He brought my father here after he bought this land. Old Master liked my father because he knew horses, and he was strong and could keep accounts, too. Knew how to make his master money. Old Master eventually made him an overseer. Best he ever had."

"I didn't know any of this, " Emilia said.

"We were too young to care about such things back then," Othello said. "I only remember some of it in a distant way. Some of the older folks—the ones that could still speak some African—would tell me bits and pieces about him as I grew. You remember old Jupiter? He knew my father back in Africa. Told me a lot about him. Jupiter took good care of me after my father was gone—that is, 'till they sold him off, too—" Othello's voice caught in his throat.

"Why'd they take your daddy away?" Emilia asked in a quiet voice.

"Commerce," he said, gripping the handle of the scythe. "When Old Master died, Marse Brabanzio wanted even more money. He decided to stud my father out to other plantations, make him a breeder. A lot of money in that, especially for a full-blooded African. My father refused to be used that way, to be debased, had too much dignity for that. So, they beat him and made him work in the fields with the field hands he used to oversee. When that didn't break him, they sold him and my momma off in different directions. Couple of years later, Marse Brabanzio sold off Jupiter, too. I didn't have anyone after that. Why do you think your folks never let you play with me anymore? Because in everyone's eyes, I was the disgraced son of the master's favorite who'd forgotten his place." Othello held the blade of the scythe up between him and Emilia. "This is the tool my father used when they put him out in the fields, before they sold him and my momma away."

Emilia took the tool from Othello and placed it back on the barrel. She took Othello's face in both hands and kissed him. "I'm sorry, Othello," she whispered through the tears that fell between their lips, "I didn't know…"

After a moment, Othello gently pushed Emilia away and stood. "If I had not done what I did to your uncle before Marse Brabanzio saw the split in his prize horse's hoof, he would have had *every* stable hand, *every* man and boy who works the barns sorely beaten. But when Marse came out for his morning ride and saw your uncle already bleeding in the dirt, that I had preempted his wrath, he was satisfied. I learned this from my father. Was why everyone hated him, too. But as long as you have me, there's no need for Marse Brabanzio to hire an overseer from the outside, some vicious drunkard or scoundrel who would get pleasure from taking out his life's disappointments on *all* of the blacks, someone who would run the plantation into the ground and create even greater misery."

Emilia wiped away tears. "No, I certainly wouldn't want to see you leave us."

She moved to embrace Othello, but he took her by the shoulders and held her back. "You should go—I expect Iago to come assist me soon with preparing the horses for the Master's ride tomorrow. Wouldn't be good for your husband to see you here with me."

"Iago? Tonight?"

"Yes," Othello said, "he'll likely be here soon. You best use the other door."

A pained smile spread across Emilia's face. "Then I should be wary of my light." She extinguished its glow, leaving them in the dimmer light of Othello's overhanging lamp. Emilia took her own and disappeared into the darkness toward the back of the barn.

"Thank you for bringing this back to me," Othello called out as he picked up the scythe and held it under the shine of his lamp.

"You may yet find a use for it," came Emilia's reply from the darkness.

Othello heard the sound of a heavy door groan shut.

He stared at the long, crescent-shaped blade. "Nothing but a long, lost memory." He rested it on the barrel and turned to the Andalusian, its head perched over the top of its stall door. Othello rubbed its muzzle. "You keep the secrets of this kingdom, do you not, great Jerusalem?"

The horse gave a contented snort at Othello's touch.

"I must prepare for our next visitor, friend." Othello went to the door and unlatched it, sliding it open just far enough to exit into the night.

A moment later, Iago appeared from the darkness deep at the back of the barn. He sneered. "Othello! Foul adulterer! How I hate you for stealing everything from me—my wife, my station, my dignity!" Iago picked up the scythe from the barrel and ran the palm of his hand along the curve of its steel blade. "I *will* find my vengeance!"

Something crashed outside the barn. Iago gasped and returned the scythe to the barrel before dashing back into the darkness of the barn.

ACT III

Othello took his time washing up from his day of working in the west fields. When he returned to the barn, Desdemona was sitting on a stack of hay bales beneath the dim glow of his lantern.

"Hello, love." Desdemona smiled as she reclined on the cushion of bundled hay, and the skirt of her elegant blue dress rode up past her ankle, revealing the creamy, white skin of her legs. She had already taken off her shoes, further revealing unblemished, slender feet with high bridges. She smiled when she noticed Othello looking at her exposed skin. "Why are you so hesitant? Come over here."

Othello knew—had always known—the danger of being with

Desdemona. But what could he do? She had been there when Jupiter was sold away, the only one to show him affection. Too much affection.

He crossed the room and knelt, taking Desdemona's ankle in one hand, sliding the other up the back of her calf to her knee. She shuddered in his hands. This was how she liked to begin.

"I was starting to think you hadn't seen my candles. You've always been here before me," Desdemona said, grinning down at Othello as he held her in his hands.

"I wanted to wash up before you got here."

She laughed. "That's okay, I kind of liked the surprise. But..." Desdemona leaned forward and took Othello's head in her hands. She planted her face in his soft hair and breathed deeply. "You know I like the way you smell before you wash—I like the sweat."

Othello's hands slid up her legs, cupping her upper thighs as she tilted his head back and leaned down further for a kiss.

He turned away at the last moment.

"What's the matter?" Desdemona purred as she nibbled at his ear.

Othello burned as he knelt between Desdemona's legs, gripping her thighs, but he couldn't stop thinking about the past, his family... Emilia.

For the first time in a long while, he considered the danger he put himself in every time he met with his master's daughter. A slave caught talking to her without averting his eyes and bowing his head would earn a brutal beating, but...*this*. Othello recalled bringing up his fears in the past, but Desdemona had just laughed. She seemed to enjoy the danger.

"Othello..." Desdemona turned his head back to face her. "Why are you so doleful?"

"I'm sorry, but I can't..."

"Are you sick?"

Othello stood and stepped away, leaving Desdemona lying on her back, empty legs spread apart. He looked away. "This is...wrong."

Desdemona sat forward with an amused sigh. "So, we're back to moralizing our love?"

"What love? This is dangerous! Not just to me, but you as well—what if your father discovered us?"

"After all these years? Please..."

"What if you turned up with a swollen belly? A black child would ruin you, destroy us both."

Desdemona laughed again. "You think I'm a little girl? I know the rhythms of my own body—and I know women in the village who take care of such things when they happen. You think I'm the first lady to lay with her father's property? You and I will have no black babies, Othello, I can assure you."

Something inside Othello's stomach turned. "You haven't..." he hesitated, his face beginning to burn. "Tell me you haven't..."

"No, love, I've never had a need for their services."

Othello relaxed, but the knot in his stomach remained as he entertained the thought of being forever entangled with Desdemona. If nothing else, he wished to be free of her demands on him.

"Stop moping around and come to me," Desdemona commanded in a playful tone. "Don't make me force you."

Othello turned to eye Desdemona as she lay on the hay bale. "And how would that be?"

"A single word."

"You would murder me with a false accusation?" Othello hissed. "How would you explain being here in the first place?"

"Easy—I have riding horses, too: I was concerned for my poor Bianca over there in her stall after this morning's fiasco with old Saul. I just *couldn't* sleep without checking on her. And then"—Desdemona pouted, and sniffed as if to hold back tears—"and then!" She fell from the hay bale to her knees, reaching into the air as if in supplication, "Oh, Daddy!" She prostrated herself on the straw-covered floor, weeping.

Othello's stomach turned again. "You speak of love, then turn and plot my murder—I am already killed in your mind!"

Desdemona's crying turned to raucous laughter. Othello had never heard such a sound from his lover. "You see, I have always been the one in charge," she said. "Whether it be my father, you, or anyone else who thinks they have control, I've arranged things so that I will always have the upper hand."

The blade of his father's scythe glinted in the dim lamplight in his periphery. That 'something' inside him bent a little.

"But I would never do anything like that," she continued, her voice quieter, her eyes softened. "Whether you believe me or not, I do love you, Othello." Desdemona stood and went to Othello, who turned away from her. She slipped her arms around him from behind and pressed her hands against his chest, pulling him to her. "You do believe me, don't you?"

"You took me as your plaything at such a young age," Othello said. "You were older—so beautiful! I felt like you were the only one who cared about me after old Jupiter was sold away."

"I did care! And haven't we kept such wonderful secrets together?"

"After tonight's performance, I can't say."

"I'm sorry," Desdemona said, resting her cheek between his shoulder blades. "I'm not myself tonight. Some things are going to change, Othello—*big* changes... I was engaged this morning."

Othello went numb. For a moment, he felt like he might teeter and fall.

Hands still pressed to his chest, Desdemona felt Othello's heartbeat quicken. "He's the son of my father's old friend from Harvard—you know what Harvard is, right? It'll be a proper—and profitable—union."

Othello groaned. He released himself from Desdemona's embrace and sat on the hay bales, head in his hands again.

"I knew you still loved me," Desdemona said. "I could feel it."

"Where will your husband take you?" Othello asked.

"North Carolina."

Then I am free, Othello thought to himself. But a terrible agony tore at him. A hot raking in his gut. His throat was so tight, he could barely breathe. He was twelve when Desdemona came to him, the only woman he had ever known intimacy with, the only woman she'd *allowed* him to be with. He groaned again as he fought against the conflicting emotions swirling within. He wanted to be glad—to be rid of the shame and fear she brought on him, to perhaps start building a new life, however limited it might be as a slave on that damnable plantation, without her lurking presence.

"Then we are finished," Othello said. "When do you leave for your new home?"

Desdemona cupped his cheeks in her hands. "Not *me*, Othello —*we*."

"What do you mean?"

"I could never leave without *you*," Desdemona said, "so I've arranged with my father for you to be a part of my dowry—isn't that wonderful, Othello?" Desdemona spun around with joy as she clapped her hands.

"You're taking me with you?"

"Yes."

"Away from here? From the plantation?"

"I knew you'd be surprised!"

"But I can't go, I can't leave this place," Othello said, trying to make sense of what leaving the plantation—the only home he had ever known—would mean. "Who would manage the place, who would be overseer?"

"Poor Othello," Desdemona said, still giddy, "this must be a lot for you to take in all at once. Look at it this way: would you rather be my father's slave or *my* servant?" Desdemona finished her question with a curtsey.

"Who will look after the others?"

"You shouldn't worry. I'm sure my handmaid's husband, Iago, would make a fine overseer—"

The name brought Othello to his feet. "Iago!"

"Yes, Iago. I gave Father the suggestion and he took to it well. Ha, ha! The handmaid and the slave-driver—wouldn't that be a fine pairing!"

"Iago! He will run this place to the ground!" A thought occurred to Othello. "So, you won't be taking Emilia with you?"

"Oh, no, I wouldn't split them up. Just you, a couple of footmen, a horse, and some other property."

His head reeling, Othello balanced himself against the barrel. "Your family has taken everything from me! My mother, my father, my dignity—even old Jupiter—"

"Stop it," Desdemona commanded. "I've been good to you,

Othello. I've given you my love, and I've never allowed anything to stand between the two of us, nothing! Not even Jupiter!"

"What was that?" Othello stared at Desdemona, his head suddenly spinning, "What of Jupiter?"

"I couldn't have you with him in the way, love. He saw everything, the clever old goat, and I couldn't have that, so I had Father send him away. So, stop this nonsense and come—"

Othello plunged the blade of the scythe deep into the base of Desdemona's neck. How it got into his hand, he could not recall, but the impact knocked the air out of Desdemona, causing her to choke. A thin collar of blood welled around the blade before sliding down Desdemona's pale chest, soaking into the intricate white lace on the front of her dress.

Desdemona stared at Othello with unbelieving eyes. She tried to speak, but nothing came out.

Blood arced through the air when Othello wrenched the curved blade from her neck. His hand hit the lantern overhead. It reeled and spun, casting the pair in violently alternating light and darkness.

Desdemona staggered backward, grasping at her neck as Othello brought the blade down again, hacking into the crease between her neck and shoulder, the weapon disappearing as he cut through flesh and bone. Her clavicle was barely an obstacle, the scythe slicing down until it was buried in her sternum. Desdemona stumbled to the ground, taking Othello with her, still grasping the scythe's wooden handle.

Hot blood sprayed from the gaping wound in her torso, drenching Othello as he struggled to pull the scythe from her body. It finally came free and he fell backward. He stood quickly, looking down at Desdemona as she crawled insensibly one way, then another, holding the gaping chasm between her neck and shoulder. She slipped in the muck her blood had formed, and she fell into it face first. Othello watched as she rolled onto her back and stared up at him, wide-eyed. She reached for him, her hand covered in blood and mud. Her lips moved, but all that came out was a gurgling, red bubble.

Othello took Desdemona's hand and held it.

After a moment, he took in a slow, deep breath, not knowing how long he'd been holding it. The lantern swung slowly, casting a strange, oscillating shadow, eclipsing then revealing Desdemona's corpse over and over again. Othello looked at his own bloody hands and wept.

A crash from the darkness made Othello leap to his feet. "Who is it?" he called into the dark. He stalked into the gloom, and returned to the light dragging Iago by his collar.

Iago struggled until Othello threw him down next to Desdemona's body. He screamed as his arm fell across the wreck of his former mistress.

Othello slapped him into silence. "Villain! Spy!"

"You've murdered Miss Desdemona! You've doomed all of us!"

"Be quiet," Othello said, setting the blade against Iago's neck. "How did you know I was here tonight? Why were you spying on me?"

The words tumbled out before he could catch himself, "Emilia told me about the signal Mis Desdemona has for you, the three candles! I came to see for myself—"

"Emilia knew?" Othello looked at the scythe in his hand. "Then perhaps she also knew about the engagement, and the arrangement to take me away..." He pushed Iago back into the blood-soaked dirt and stood. "She put the means for salvation in my hands and trusted me to find a way!"

"What will you do now?" Iago asked, groveling at Othello's feet.

"What will *we* do, you mean. You're going to help me sink her body in the river. Stay here while I get what we need from the tack room." Othello shook the scythe at Iago until he swallowed hard and nodded.

Othello disappeared into the tack room where most of the riding equipment was stored. Iago heard him rummaging around, making a ruckus. He looked back at Desdemona's body and shivered.

As he struggled to control his fear, a thought struck him. He reached into his pocket and retrieved the lace sleeve Emilia gave to him, the hand-me-down from Desdemona. He wiped the sleeve in the pooling blood, then slipped it behind a stack of barrels. He muttered, "When your father finds this, Miss Desdemona, he will recognize his daughter's undergarment, and Othello will have to make account of himself for tonight, I will make sure of it! Then we will have our vengeance on this false prince, and I shall have my reward!" Iago quickly returned to his position by Desdemona's body.

※

Othello returned pushing a large wheelbarrow filled with horse blankets, ropes, and sacks of horseshoes. He ordered Iago to help him roll Desdemona into one of the wide blankets and truss her tightly with rope. Once she was bound like a monstrous cocoon, they scrubbed and washed the floor and anywhere else possibly stained by blood. They spread fresh straw from the hay loft and inspected the barn, ensuring nothing was missed.

"Help me wrap Desdemona in a second blanket so she doesn't seep a trail as we carry her to the river. We'll use the bags of horseshoes to weigh her down."

Iago did as he was told and spread the thick blanket on the freshly cleaned floor. Once the blanket was fully extended, Othello struck him from behind, burying the scythe deep in Iago's back. Iago yelped, but before he could scream, Othello planted his foot on his back and forced him to the ground. Othello yanked the blade, unmooring it.

Iago landed in the middle of the padded horse blanket, only managing a moan before Othello grabbed him by the forehead and slid the crescent blade across and into his throat. He dropped Iago's severed head next to his body and stood. "I can't leave a witness, dear Iago—especially you, my enemy and rival." Othello rolled Iago's body in the second horse blanket and bound it into another tight cocoon.

After giving the barn one more inspection for any errant blood, Othello loaded the cocoons into the wheelbarrow. He paused for a moment over his handiwork before extinguishing the lantern and rolling the monstrous cargo out of the barn and into the night.

ACT IV

BRABANZIO PLANTATION, BELL COUNTY, TEXAS, 1856—DAY

By noon the next day, the Brabanzio house was a flurry of anxious activity. Desdemona was missing. By mid-afternoon, Brabanzio had ordered his most trusted servants to conduct a thorough search of the entire plantation. It was to be led by his overseer, Othello.

An hour before sunset, Brabanzio ordered Othello to assemble his every servant and slave out by the west field. He had become manic with fear for his daughter's well-being and had gathered a posse of men from nearby Salado.

Othello paced at the head of the large group of fellow slaves—men, women, their children, mothers carrying infants and toddlers, the elderly. Every slave was present, including the house servants. Among them all, Othello stood out, a head taller than everyone and powerfully built, he carried a large cudgel as a symbol of his elevated position. A cowskin whip hung from a strap at his side like a coiled viper. His father's scythe swung from a leather strap at his other hip.

He stopped pacing to watch a dozen men riding horses along a foot trail, cutting through the middle of the wheat field. The sun was setting behind them, and Othello reflected that it was almost time for the harvest.

"Othello!" The voice brought him back to the moment. He found Emilia huddled with the house servants, wringing her hands with worry. "I don't see Iago. Have you seen my husband today?"

Othello shrugged. "I have not. I fear for him when he is found." He turned back at the rumbling of hoofbeats. "Hey, now," he called at the horses' approach, pointing his cudgel at the assembly behind him. "Tighten up. For Marse Brabanzio!"

The line of horses came to a stop in front of the assembly, Desdemona's father, Josiah Brabanzio, at its head. Although he edged toward his senior years, he was vigorous in health. His collar was uncharacteristically undone, and Othello noted that he still wore his morning coat, the Colt revolver he used as an officer in the Mexican War tucked beneath in a leather holster. "Ho, Othello," he shouted from atop Jerusalem. "Everyone accounted for?"

"All except one, Marse Brabanzio," Othello said, bowing his head. "Iago is yet to be found."

"Iago? But how could this be?"

"Even the most trustworthy slave can take advantage of a chaotic situation and run off, good sir," said a young man on a blue roan. Othello had never seen him before. A tall, slender man of elegant dress and a pencil mustache.

Brabanzio spat in frustration. "We'll deal with that later. Othello! Have you questioned everyone?"

"Yes, Marse—but no one has seen anything of Miss Desdemona."

"No one? So, none of you bastards has seen my daughter?" Brabanzio bellowed over the assembly.

"Take care, Marse," Othello said. "We'll all search the grounds through the night! We will find Miss Desdemona."

"See to it," Brabanzio nodded, seemingly calmed by Othello's assurances.

A pair of riders from another direction rode up to Brabanzio and the stranger. They brought their rides to an abrupt stop, both men ashen, their eyes wide with shock.

"Mister Brabanzio," one of them said, reaching into his coat, "we've found something." He pulled out a piece of fabric. A bloody lace sleeve.

Emilia averted her gaze and began to weep as the rest of the assembly gasped and chattered. Brabanzio took the bloody sleeve from the rider and moaned, sagging in his saddle. Othello looked on, constrained.

"What has happened?" Brabanzio howled.

"We found it in the barn, sir," the rider said.

"Are you sure it's Desdemona's garment?" the stranger asked, placing a consoling hand on Brabanzio's shoulder.

"I know it well," Brabanzio said through his tears, "I bought the dress this sleeve belongs to for her in England..." He caressed the sleeve, then looked at it more closely. "And I know that she wore it happily for many years"—his tone changed—"before giving it away…"

Brabanzio looked up with a fierce stare, searching the crowd. He found who he sought and pointed. "Desdemona gave this sleeve to you, Emilia! Othello, take her!"

Emilia screamed as she fell to her knees, weeping desperately. Othello turned, stricken by the order given him. Emilia jerked as Othello took her by the wrist. "Othello, no! Do not do this!"

"Hush," he whispered, "no harm will come to you, I promise."

"Bring her here, boy," Brabanzio ordered.

Othello pulled Emilia to her feet and forced her forward. She fell prostrate in front of Brabanzio and the stranger.

"Isn't this Desdemona's handmaid?" the stranger asked. "I have seen her during my visits."

"It is, Cassio—and now she will tell us where my daughter is!"

Othello realized the stranger had to be Desdemona's fiancé. His face became flush.

"I don't know where she is, Marse Brabanzio," Emilia cried.

"Liar," Brabanzio screamed. He shook the bloody lace sleeve at her. "Did you lose this in the barn when you took her? And where is your husband?"

Emilia cried, unable to form an answer.

"This missing slave is her husband?" the elegant stranger asked. "I think we've uncovered a terrible conspiracy." He looked out at the rest of the assembly.

"Yes, we'll get the truth!" Brabanzio turned to Othello. "Strip her down and use your whip!"

Emilia screamed. Prayers and moans went up as terror spread. A perverse anticipation came from the horsemen who chattered quietly as they passed around a plug of tobacco.

"Whip her," Brabanzio ordered again.

"I will not."

There was a sudden silence throughout the yard save the sound of wheat stalks rustling in the wind.

"Othello!"

"I will not." He helped Emilia to her feet, pushed her toward the crowd of servants who hugged her into their fold.

"Othello—have you lost your senses!" Brabanzio said.

"I have finally found them, my master," he said. "I will not hurt Emilia. She is innocent, I know it."

"How can you know such a thing?"

"I know it."

"Beware, sir, lest you lose control," the elegant stranger said. "I need not tell you this."

"Save your words, I won't be budged," Othello said. "I've forfeited all family and virtue in your service, but I refuse to falter further. Emilia is innocent of any crime."

Brabanzio leapt from his horse and advanced on Othello. "Give me that, you bastard," he cried, fumbling for the whip at Othello's side. There was a ruckus from the slaves and the riders as Othello fought with Brabanzio. The struggle was brief, as Othello grabbed his master by the throat and threw him to the ground. Brabanzio cowered in the dirt when Othello pulled the scythe from his belt and raised it high.

A gunshot rang out. Everything went silent again.

Othello staggered backward, dropping the scythe. A red bloom spread across the front of his shirt. He looked up to see Cassio, the stranger, pointing a revolver at him.

"Are you alright, sir?" Cassio asked Brabanzio.

"Yes," he replied in a daze, staring up at Othello. The stranger holstered his pistol.

Othello fell to his knees. He swayed slightly, holding a hand over his bloody chest. He looked at Emilia weeping. Their eyes met.

He smiled. "No way but this; killing myself, to die upon a kiss…"

Othello fell.

Only the wheat rustling and quiet weeping made any sound. One of the horsemen spat some chaw.

Brabanzio crawled over and put a hand on Othello's ankle. A strange reverie came over him. After a moment, he stood and mounted his horse. "There are no answers here. Cato," he called to a house servant, "see that this is cleaned up. You're in charge out here for now." Brabanzio rode toward the mansion, the rest of his entourage close behind.

Emilia ran to Othello. She fell to her knees and pulled his head into her lap. She wailed as the rest of the assembly gathered around her.

"In my design to keep you near, dear Othello, I have killed *both* the men I love!"

Several women came and lifted Emilia from her place, consoling her, as she continued to weep.

Cato stepped forward. "Who will help me bear Othello's body away?"

A dozen men, from both the house and the fields, lifted Othello onto their shoulders. Cato led them away in a solemn procession toward the slaves' quarters.

The yard was empty until a young boy, not more than eight—whose name is remembered only in one of Brabanzio's inventory ledgers—ran to the abandoned scythe and picked it up. He wiped tears from his eyes as he looked the scythe over, turning it carefully in his hands. It was clean, except for strange markings he could not read. A reddish stain highlighted the marks, making them stand out against the light-colored wood. The boy took the scythe in one hand and turned toward the mansion. He crouched in a defensive position and slashed the scythe to his left.

"I will not!"

He advanced another step and swung the blade against a second imaginary foe.

"I will not!"

The boy stood straight and held the scythe in both hands, smiling. He spun on his heels, still gripping the blade, and ran to follow the procession that bore Othello away.

THE WINDS DID SING

(THE TEMPEST)

LK KITNEY

The rains had begun the day before, building in strength with the winds—like ghosts screaming for release. Blue-white lightning laced the sky finer than the deadliest silks spiders wove, the ship in the turbulent gray waters as snared by the light as a fly to the web.

Prospero—who had clung to the title of duke as if his old standing was relevant on this lonely isle—watched the scene, unable to look away. The striking light was pale as the bleached bone of his skull. His empty sockets drank in the rain and wind howled through the space where his mind had been.

He did not watch alone. His daughter sat beside him on the rock, where the son of a witch had once been kept, knees to her chest against the deluge. Miranda wore her father's once fine cloak—of green wool and golden threads—over her shoulders. His staff lay in danger of being swept away in the rain-rivers at her bare feet, the power within it subdued.

Waves full of drowning fury struck the ship as it disappeared behind walls of water and violent spume—the raging spittle of Miranda's own dread desires. She was too far to hear the shrieking of timbers or the cries of sailors as the water sought its tribute. The bright yellow and red flag the ship flew was only visible in the flashes, each time more tattered until it tore free, and was lost.

"I promised thee, father. No standard of Naples shall sail these waters," she said, looking down on the duke's smooth dome. She could almost hear his despair carried on the air with the screaming of the wind and the weeping of the rain, but that was illusion. Her victory was as hollow as the cavern behind his eye sockets.

Miranda unclenched her fist, imprints of nails against the soft flesh of her palm, and granted the water its desire. It rose and consumed the ship. She would get her tithe for her generosity: driftwood to burn, supplies washed ashore, bodies for fat and bone—the way the witch's son had taught her.

Cal had taught her so many things.

Miranda, come...

As children, Miranda, Cal—then still the witch's daughter—and his mother, Sycorax, who loved this lost island, knew its plants and animals, and called it home—would take to the fresh springs and brine pits, where they gathered water and berries, fish and crabs. Cal had shown Miranda how to trap and skin small animals, and she would anchor him well against the cliffs to keep him from falling in their searches for birds and eggs. Miranda perfected the harvests, raking the bounty from the wild hazelnut trees, and Cal would root for pignuts, before they had learned to better bend the land to their needs. Survival wrapped in child's play.

Initially, as if sisters, they were rarely separated save on nights where the moon hung heavy and full. Cal and his mother would go to a secret place and not return until dawn. Miranda hated those nights. She would scowl and sulk, a match for Prospero who—like the black night around the silver light—would mutter curses at the witch's absence and her heathen ways. Then, he would read to Miranda from his books, invoking words of power and command that sent shivers down her spine as their fire flickered gold and red against the walls. Or, he would tell her of where they had come, and Miranda's part in his plans to return to glory and wealth, disregarding her own budding desires in the face of his need. Rock, inside and out.

But rock weathers and crumbles in the onslaught of wind and water, whose dreams were small but not to be ignored.

In turn, Prospero would demand Miranda travel alone with him on nights where there was no moon at all. They would go to the shores to watch his beacon fires flare; the light of his hopes swallowed by the empty void with no more accompaniment than the sound of soft surf, whispering breezes, and his desperate weeping.

Miranda, come...

The winds themselves called to her. She would dance as the witch's son had taught her.

Miranda left her father to witness Apollo's chariot skipping over the surface of her fading storm. The last warmth from the heels of his fiery steeds prickled against the cold rain on her skin as she returned to the cave she had once called home, ready to make preparations. She hung the sodden cloak from a finger trapped within the stone, nothing but rock. It wore a hole through the weaving of golds and greens—a blending of seasons that should never have been. Much like Prospero himself.

At Miranda's will, the dying embers of a fire—crimson against ash—took root. Fed with logs brought to dry under the new moon, they were dark and empty of promise. It was safest to avoid promise in spark and flame. It was too presumptuous, not knowing its place. It would leap from hearth to heart and burn free, fed on blood and passion.

As the flames surged for her, surrounded by history, memories continued to creep in like fog. The storm outside may have been abating, but the one that had caused it—the anger nestled in her heart—was harder to see dissipate. Better to let it thunder than bring it to the dance and lay it before the queen.

All Miranda knew of that fire-born frenzy had been her father's subtle fear of it when his attempts to bring Cal to heel had failed, the boy's wild spirit refusing to be contained by the restraints of a land he had never known.

"*Thou dost desire a lady's maid, but sir, I am no maid, and I am no lady,*" he had said, standing his ground one hot day when his mother was absent on business of her own.

The duke had laughed but, when Cal persisted, threatened. *"Then I shall work thee like a man."*

The morning past that next full moon, Cal had returned no longer wearing the tattered dresses Miranda was used to but a rough-spun tunic and breeches. He stood tall and proud, his hair shorn. As the moons passed, his form had shifted from that of a young working woman to the solid leanness of an active young man, and the way he looked at Miranda began to change too.

It was then that her father's fear had become apparent—when Cal had explained what Miranda's father and Sycorax would do when the children had been absent. Cal had offered the same to Miranda, content to wait for seasons to rise and fall, greens and oranges shifting with the island's slow breathing through the passage of years until, and only if, Miranda would allow it. Such permission would have been denied her as a gentlewoman but, since he had become the witch's son, Cal could not follow his mother. There would need to be a new witch, and a witch made her own rules.

Prospero, fearing that permission would come too soon, sent them to their chores separately: Cal, far from home and Miranda close, watched at all times. But they were still little more than children and, once their chores were complete, he could not keep them from playing together—a balm against the way the adults would raise their voices at each other.

"I shall not allow thee to corrupt her with thine heathen ways. She is my way out of this prison. They will not take her in if she does not reflect the culture of the trained noblewoman she rightly is."

"Bah," Sycorax would return with equal ire. *"You would hobble her to a stranger; imprison her in a land she doth not know for thine own freedom? I took thee for misguided, old man, I did not take thee for cruel."*

Miranda would beg Cal to never speak to her that way. He would nod, as serious as the face of the witch looking out over the island when she thought herself unobserved. Then he would grin and give chase, their games resumed, childish laughter as wicked and wild as the spirits Miranda was yet to learn to see.

Miranda, come...

Spirits. Only one spirit called the cave where her father's books lay abandoned home. Usually at his place against the wall, beside the duke's cloak, trapped in a knotted branch of pine whittled into a staff, he was conspicuous by his absence.

Left beside Prospero, overlooking the sea. Dreaded mistake.

"Well met, sister," the spirit whispered when she returned to the rock and took up the staff, swallowing the way it made her stomach turn.

"Thou art not my brother, Ariel. Poison to my father's ears, thou shall not have mine."

"Then brevity suffices. Thou should return me to the cave, before this cell, storm-bitten as it is, rots through and undoes thine fine work on me." His shape inside the branch flowed along the grain of the wood, striving for the surface, longing to be as free as wildfire. As untrustworthy as breaks between spring rains.

"Malignant thing. What art thee planning?" Miranda asked but, whether from the tightness of her grip or the spirit's fancy, he only shared whisper-soft echoes of animals in pain.

It was a better sound than his delight, heard only twice. Both times came scarlet-drenched and full of grief.

The first had been on a night like this: rain-soaked summer warmth that washed the night clean for the full moon following Miranda's new bloods.

In secret, Sycorax had dressed Miranda in a floral crown and a worm-spun gown before taking her by one hand and her son by the other. They had moved as shadows to wash at a quiet spring before reaching a glade where the moon and her stars basked dark grass and night-shrouded trees in bright argent.

Naiads in reed crowns had slipped like stream-currents between the trees, dancing around moonbeams. Men of shadow, whose hats kept the light from their faces, carried sickles of a waxing moon over their shoulders and bowed for the hands of the water women. Together, they trailed silver and silken tails.

Those beings had not seemed like the spirits in her father's books, but many beautiful things could be deceptive: the deep blue swirls of riptides or the bright colors of frogs whose touch would bring death.

"Be not afeared," Sycorax had said, seeing Miranda's awe. *"The isle is*

full of sounds, and sweet airs that give delight and hurt not. To see and conjure them is thine power, yet dormant. Until it awakens, hush and be mute, else our spell is marred."

"And if I do not wish for such power?"

"The choice is thine, Miranda. But true choice requires options. Thou must know what thee may have." The witch had spoken with a distant look that suggested an ambition Miranda could not yet fathom.

Any concern had faded as Cal led her to join the dancers.

The warmth of his arms as he led her through steps had banished the cold gazes of the moon-queen and her consort, buried under the weight of his bushel. No sickle for the king, though he wore a long knife as silvery as his wife as she stepped between the clouds, treading across stars.

"Witch, thine ways with thine own child I could tolerate, but thou dost not have leverage with my daughter." Prospero blew into the clearing and broke the spell, the spirits less substantial in the face of his unwelcome presence.

Gold streaks flitted between the dancers, fire amid the frost and—like fire—the gold caught, sparking against the silver moon. Miranda had clutched her stomach against rising bile as the nymphs and their reapers writhed. They did not scream, though their faces twisted in agony as their forms contorted, faces elongating, limbs stretching to the ground. Silver sickles became snarling teeth. Silken gowns tore from hunched spines. When they rose again, they did so as beasts with golden fire in their eyes.

Cal cried out as they drove him from Miranda with wild howls—otherworldly and haunting and laced with joy at odds with the terror they inspired. The witch's glance barely shifted to seek out her son as he fled, her entire focus on Prospero.

The twisted hounds nipped at Miranda as they passed, herding her towards her father, who held her in a bruising grip, his eyes alight with that same golden fire.

"Neither dost thee, Prospero," Sycorax replied. *"The bond of father fosters responsibility, not ownership. Not in this place. Thee and thine golden whispers of discontent would do well to remember thou art far from thine courts and churches. Miranda's choices are hers to make. As are mine."*

A ribbon of gold had darted between the trees and Miranda's voice whispered, *"Lies."*

She had not spoken, her hands clasped across her silent mouth in surprise as childlike laughter echoed around the glade, laced with that raw delight the spirits had shared as they had chased Cal.

"Miranda, return home. This is not thine argument," the witch had said, breaking her fix on Prospero to smile in reassurance before returning to the man before her.

Miranda had obeyed, relieved to run from that strange laughter, to leave her father and Sycorax arguing about power and freedom and choice—their voices rising to a single scream. Then silence.

Cal waited for her at the cave, his fear a match for hers as they held each other tight, before sleeping against each other as they had waited for their parents to return—his warmth a safety.

When her father returned alone at sunrise, he had blood on his clothes and mud under his nails. His anger burned out, he said nothing as he had taken Cal by force, ignoring the struggles of both Cal and Miranda to resist or entreaty him, and had fastened the witch's son to a rock overlooking the sea, close to the crumbling cliff.

Offered no shelter from the sun or the rain, no meal besides what he could find for himself in the few hours free of his bondage: fresh-brook mussels, withered roots, and acorn husks, forbidden even fire, Cal endured a Promethean existence.

Days had become weeks, and the witch did not return. Even the sun had stayed away for the mourning of heavy rain and low clouds building as much inside Miranda as outside. Animals had gone into hiding, plants into waterlogged stupor—the island grieving.

Though years had passed since, it was still easy to grieve the witch. Especially when the memories Ariel brought forth came crawling unbidden like worms from the dirt. As deep and treacherous as winter snows.

Miranda, come...

She leaned the staff and its spirit beside her father's cloak, no time left for her usual preparations. The winds called for her. The worm-spun gown she slipped on was tired and much-mended, the floral crown almost a hat, fresh blooms interwoven against old, all wilted and brown—built on memories of moons past.

"Thou shouldst stay," Ariel whispered. "'Tis a poor night to be alone, witch."

"Then I pity thee, spirit, though thou hast earned this solitude."

There was a sigh, softer than the gentlest breeze. "If thou wish to leave me naught but the flotsam of thine anger, I shall make good use of it."

Miranda left the cave without answering, unwilling to be drawn into an argument with all her sorrows edged in gold, to serve his purpose of delaying her.

Sensing her need for haste, slips of wind pulled her forward, lifting her until she barely left footprints through the wet grass and weeds. As close to the sky as she could reach.

The spring remained a place of tranquillity; the water was like ice, even in the heat of summer. Buoyed by the spirits of the wind, she arrived with time to wash away both the tempest and the lingering emotions that had caused it. Then she settled to await the witch's son.

He would arrive at the moment the sun flashed below the horizon and no earlier. If Miranda was not waiting, Cal would leave, perhaps never to return. It was his nature, a peculiarity that persisted after Prospero's many abuses without his mother's mitigations to balance them.

Revealing an unwonted cruelty in the witch's absence, Prospero would take Cal into the island, leaving Miranda under a presence she could never quite see or hear beyond vague echoes of concerns nestled in her heart. Yet, Prospero would know if she wandered during the day. He would take his anger at her disobedience out on Cal, leaving Miranda chained, invisibly, as tightly as the witch's son to his rock, to study her father's scriptures and learn to navigate imaginary court politics.

Evenings had brought the duke's words ringing hollow on her tongue in recital, proof she had not been idle. Sometimes, they had echoed back from the cold cave wall in a voice not quite either of theirs—a golden shimmer in the corner of her eye that vanished if she sought to catch it, nothing more than fancy and firelight.

Moonless nights still meant trips to the shore, where the light of Prospero's unanswered beacons revealed the growing skeleton of a wooden ship that would carry them both to peopled lands, where he would regain his rightful status on the back of Miranda's worth.

"Thou art a daughter of Milan. It is time for thee to take a husband with influence and wealth. I shall be a duke again."

When she had asked what would become of Cal in those dreams of her father's, he would not answer—her words falling on ears given to a private glory whispered from a golden slip on the wind.

Full moons had brought weeping from the rock outside the cave and a shared grief in Miranda that had no balm, her tears silent in companionship, but that was better than startling awake in the quiet hours while her father slept, shaking off dreams of bone-white roots growing through the sodden earth to reach for her.

There had been a sense of peace in the cave in those few hours, her father's invisible sentry vanished on errands or mischief all its own. Its absence gave her the opportunity to offer the witch's son his freedom, willing to face the wrath of her father alone.

He had refused, though his bruises almost shone black in the moonlight between new and full and back again, as his body had begun to twist into new shapes under the labors Prospero demanded. *"Not alone, and thine father would scour the earth for thee, Miranda. We would always be running. That is no freedom for a witch."*

"I am no witch, Cal."

"Wouldst thou like to be?"

Witch. Nothing more than a child's game. But it had held more fancy than waiting to become a stranger's wife for her father's glory. So it became their midnight secret. When the oppressive pall left the cave, Cal had taught Miranda his mother's knowledge—things she had taught him before the truth of his masculinity had limited his abilities: how to see beings of sunlight and wind and starshine. Simple things, eager to be noticed.

As the moon had cycled across the skies, growing lean and large as the seasons changed, and under that bright silver full of promises, he had taught her how she would see those more elusive, those who waited for her power to show before acknowledging her. In the half-moon lights and in a low voice, he would warn her of rare, belligerent spirits with malice at their core and a desire to control as a witch did.

On either side of the empty nights when Miranda had been expected on the shore, pain and bitterness would lace Cal's lessons, delivered with a short temper: how to curse with ravens feathers and toads, and the many uses of death and decay. He would whisper how to bring down the sun and use its fire for fevers.

The only thing he could not teach was how to dance. Even if Miranda had broken his bonds, it did not take a witch's vision to see how he struggled against the abuses Prospero delivered or the way his long containment was taking his form, replacing it with the soft curves of a woman. Forbidden from dancing with the moon queen and taking the boons she had bestowed that had made him true, her graces were fading and Cal—his days full of labor and his nights' rests broken by invisible torments—had woken at Prospero's command with the reluctance of one who did not wish to leave his dreams behind.

Miranda…

Cal stood in the last dappled shadows of an old yew, dressed in moon-silver, his face shadowed. He carried a sickle over his shoulder. "Greetings, witch. Care to dance?"

His voice was whisper soft, his touch—when she ran to him—light as moonbeams. He offered an arm to escort her to the glade, trees giving way to nettles, docks, and mallows with their heads bowed, heavy from the rain.

There were no nymphs, no reapers beyond the witch's son—no need for audience or spectacle.

The moon silvered the leaves of a mighty tree that had not been there on that first night, years before. Its white wood was as pitted and marred as the heavy bones of large beasts. Ebony leaves, fine as hair, drooped like fine willow and the blossoms were scraps of torn brown flesh with long, blood-red stamens. Its roots were those that had reached for Miranda in her slumber, lacing the island, holding everything together until the new witch had come into her own power under Cal's guidance.

The Sycorax tree.

The spirit of the old witch, contained within, had long since faded like mist under the heat of day—dormant in a place from which she would not easily wake—but Miranda still brushed a hand against the dry wood and laid a flower from her crown at the feet of the once mighty witch. The echoes under her touch were silvered blessings: to not grieve this strange bone tree in the space between life and death, but to dance as nothing but herself, with joy and love, under the moon queen. Cal kept his distance, nothing further to share with his mother after the first night he had seen her this way.

When Miranda had been unable to bear Cal's suffering from a distance any longer, she had freed him despite his caution and brought him to dance.

"*Thou art the witch, Miranda,*" he had said then, though he made no effort to move until Miranda had taken his hand. "*And I thine servant, ever. My heart is to your service and so, we shall dance.*"

His words had made her own heart fly, longing to take to the sky in elation, though she had no understanding of why as she had urged him from his perch before her father's watchful sentry returned. The sight of the tree in the clearing had made all investigation of the way her heart continued to flutter vanish.

Prospero had never spoken of what had happened to Sycorax on that night of their last fight. Though Miranda and Cal had both known the fate of Cal's mother, deep in their hearts, Miranda had held some hope of the witch's return. To find it manifest only in the witch's knowledge of plant and spirit had been hard to bear.

Under the bright light of that moon, Cal had held Miranda close, his arms a safe embrace from days spent with her father's stale books and the paranoia of observation from his sentry. At any other time, Miranda would have said Cal, silent in his loss, was a thing divine, but the guilt of finding beauty in his heartache kept Miranda quiet. Then the moment had passed—the chance lost.

She had clung to Cal as an old, familiar nausea replaced her grief. A flash of sharp gold whipped by before Prospero had snared them, like love and war, in a fishing net to drag them home.

All Miranda's power, still as soft as unfurling petals, could not stop her father as he had beat Cal across the prison rock with violent passion. A whisper of gold had sung in the new dawn in a cold, vindictive voice, giving itself away in its glee.

Unable to move her father to kindness—that same feverish light in his eyes as the night the witch died—Miranda had gone to the boat that Prospero had forced Cal to build. With a fury all her own, she had summoned the wild delight of an untamed fire and set it free until the duke's hope was nothing more than ash.

On his knees, he had howled at the ruins, the winds stirring ash and sand together. *"I must be confined here by you? To this bare isle? Thou hast not the right. Release me from my bonds, wench."*

"I am the witch, father. I am *the right of this place. And I say thee shall have no rescue. No ships, whether from your beloved Milan, Naples, or elsewhere, shall sail these waters. The winds and the water both shall betray them at my request."*

Miranda had left him cursing her name and his own sorry luck. *"My ending is despair!"*

For all his histrionics, her act would only delay him, would only invigorate his need to strip her from her home and tie her to a man with whom she shared no love. That was the only use the duke had seen for her—the extent of her worth. She would crush that dream too. She would tie herself to the man she did love, first.

Besides, stoic and uncomplaining as the rocks as he was, Cal could not have crafted a second ship the way he had the first. There was not enough of him left to give, and Miranda would not see it wasted on an old man's foolish dream.

She curled up next to the witch's son, tethered to his rock, overlooking the ocean and the distant horizon. The view was so different compared to the inky blue of night. They had held each other tight; blood, ash, and tears mixing across their skin as his heat warmed through her.

"Why dost thou stay in such a prison, Cal?"

"For thee, maid. I have space enough here, when I can behold thee."

She kissed him. *"I am your wife, if you would marry me."*

Though he had winced as he laughed, a low thing, it held no cruelty. *"I have no need for a wife, nor you for a husband. But for clarity: ay, with a heart as willing as bondage e'er of freedom. Here's my hand, forever."*

When she had kissed him again, placing his rough hands where he could feel her desire and joy in his words, it had not been the pain of the fresh beating that had made him stop. The fight for his control was one he had been close to losing as he held her still, pulling away to create cool distance between them. *"I love and want thee, Miranda, but to act in this moment would be to spite thine father most. That would only hurt us."*

He may have said more, but bellowing like an old bull announced Prospero's return from his misery. Though her father had only roared, his face red with fury, his voice whispered in Miranda's ear that her plans were doomed to fail. That, without Cal's heathen blessings at their full strength, she could not be devalued by him, no matter all their pretty words of bonding—as if her heart had no value of its own. She could not fight that she was to be traded for Milan, or Naples.

Before she could answer, Prospero himself had reached her as his voice faded into the winds with sickening laughter. Cal had yelled as Prospero pulled Miranda from the rock and threw her to the ground.

She stared, dazed, at the sun fringed in a golden halo that resolved into a pointed face—the approximation of a man—full of malice before it vanished, leaving the sun as it always was. Her unease had made her pause to swallow before she saw the men wrestling, Cal's tethers never properly fastened in Prospero's eagerness to hurt him.

The duke's head had bounced off stone after a violent shove, scarlet seeping through his graying hair. He had stumbled towards the cliffs, his unrelenting vice-grip pulling at Cal in his imbalance while the golden wind had laughed, childlike, from all directions.

Miranda had blinked, and the three men were gone, almost soundlessly. Only the soft crunch of loosened gravel knocking against the cliff as it fell to the earth too was any indication of what had happened.

It had not been her father Miranda called out for as she saw the remains of her heart dashed to the ground so far down, framed in blood red and brown stone, still arm-in-arm with her father, soon to be taken by the tides.

Years later, once she was strong enough to ask, the sea had returned what it could of Prospero's coral-hoary bones, lying five fathoms down—his skull alone, pearls where his eyes had been.

Cal kissed her hand, breaking her free of the memories that haunted her from the moment the west winds had warned of that wretched ship.

"Thou lingers too long in the past, witch. I did not come here for thine sorrow. I know that too well already," Cal said. His touch was no longer warm, but his smile rang true; as familiar as the sight of home, or the sliver of bright silver she would sometimes see streaking through the night sky, reveling in his eternity of freedom. To him, the winds. A spirit, yes, but the most pleasing to Miranda's eye.

She longed for the weight of him to ground her, root her deep in the earth with him until the misery passed—until the way Ariel's entreaties had left a slick across her heart and mind like oil faded—safe in his company. She returned his smile as best she could.

Safe in company.

Under the blessing of the moon-queen and her consort, nymphs and reapers joined the fray as the witch and the winds danced, starlight in their eyes, in her tears at all the lost chances. Tears for her love, fleeting and distant—as impossible to keep as a sigh.

It was never enough but, for Miranda's sake, Cal had already endured much. That they danced was his choice, not her request. One night, he would choose to visit no more; on a whim, or Miranda's absence. That made these nights all the more precious. It was foolish to mar them with tears and concerns that had not come to pass, though the dread tore at her, twisting and coiling like snakes, rising with venom before subsiding.

It was still as strong as that first lonely, lonely, day when Miranda had tucked herself between the roots of the witch-tree, feeling the old witch's power offering one last boon to ease a heartbreak without end —to mollify a new witch before she grew twisted in her pain. The old bone tree had given her the knowledge of the golden spirit that had corrupted her father and led to all Miranda's sorrows, and how to imprison him.

Though it had taken almost a year, Miranda had done so. It had been taxing, despite her most unmitigable rage. Her father's staff was barely adequate, but it was a prison she could maintain. Ariel would not find freedom so easily again.

Curse that malignant thing, gold amongst the silver. It would not give her peace, even confined. Cal, his shadowed face hiding his thoughts—as much as a spirit had them—unable to do more than watch as Miranda crashed to her knees, cramps of a bitter wrongness tearing through her insides: hot iron claws and acid.

"Well met, sister," came a whispery voice woven between the crackle of red fire. A form with shadow and shape approached the glade, leaving imprints where spirits would not. A man dressed in fine clothes. He held a torch made from a pine staff aloft.

Ariel, in the form of a thin, pointed man, strained to be free of the burning remains of Prospero's staff in the stranger's hand. No peace, indeed. "I must thank thee, witch, for the jetsam of thine anger. I promised thee I would make good use of it," Ariel said, his glee evident as the staff burned past his shoulders and across his chest, his power growing as his prison failed. "This prince jumped before thou gave his ship to the sea, and so was no part of thine bargain with the ocean or the winds. That makes him mine, and the ears of men are so easy to bend."

The prince stood in a stupor, listening to something Miranda could not hear, before the golden spirit turned its attention back to her, his thin face twisted into hateful joy. "I remember the words of thine father's books, child," Ariel whispered. "I do so like 'thou shalt not suffer a witch to live.' For the suffering I have endured from thee, it seems a fine balance." His voice rose. "Rabble of this place, I incite thee to quick motion."

The long grass heads weighted with seed, which had tickled Miranda's ankles as she'd danced, wrapped around her legs and held her to the ground. She reached behind her for the safe silver of the witch's son, but he struggled against the white bones of his mother's embrace —the last traces of the old witch too weak to fight Ariel's influence— as the pine staff burned away.

An exchange of captivity Miranda could not allow.

The grasses, entwined with white bone roots, traced up her calves and over her thighs as the spirit behind her father's malice laughed—as raw and wild as the times it had provoked action from Prospero's dark heart.

The nymphs and reapers had vanished in the firelight, and the queen was nothing more than the moon—too distant to do more than watch the struggle between witch and spirit as Miranda urged the spirits of grass and witch-tree to bend to her instead. But, no matter how strong the witch, one of their own held more sway.

The witch-tree wrapped around Miranda's waist, roots digging through her skin until white bone was stained red.

Ariel was free almost to his knees, stretching like a cat. With the last breaths allowed by the roots tightening around her ribs, Miranda turned to the prince who, in his strange repose—eyes wide open, yet asleep—ignored the heat of his pine staff torch that blistered the skin on his hands and singed his fine clothes.

The golden fire of Miranda's nightmares shone in his dazed eyes as he put the torch down, careful not to extinguish it. "Thou shalt not suffer a witch to live," he said in a flat voice in answer to her pleas.

Cal was nothing more than a familiar sense in the heart of the bone-tree. Trapped. He would never be the winds again. Miranda could do nothing as the prince broke off a sharp branch and drove it through her chest with the clumsy effort of a man unused to labor.

One dead witch to kill another.

Miranda had no air left to cry out, but Ariel screamed in delight, his laughter ringing through the glade as the prince picked up the torch again.

Moon-frost through dry bone wood, the old witch was nothing more than an echo of a once great power, given to the sun and the rain and the earth. The power of life over death. Of growth. She was her own failed attempt to contain Ariel within herself, from the night Prospero had killed her. Miranda had to make the same attempt before Ariel slipped into the world by poisoning the mind of the hapless prince the way he had Prospero.

Alone, the old witch had failed. But Miranda had the last blessings and the knowledge of the Sycorax tree, and Cal's heart coursing through the sap of the tree entwined with her own, lending her his strength.

With arms heavier than stone, the new witch reached to her crown.

THE WINDS DID SING

A twig of oak leaf and acorn fell at the prince's feet, to sit in the mash of blood and dirt.

Stuck to the earth, Miranda dug her toes into the loam, where they stretched like roots of their own, feeding on the life that ran through the island. Strength from growth moved up her trunk until silver bark shone through the white bones of another woman's magic.

Ariel tried to pull his feet from the last of Prospero's staff, his golden fire filling Miranda's dimming vision. His narrow face looked down on her with devious delight.

She grinned to match, feeling her face twist and droop, as she urged the spirit of the oak tree nestled in the acorn's heart to share this growth with her and be nourished, for a favor.

A green shoot burst from the ground and wrapped around the dazed prince. Ariel's screams of victory were touched with fear as the staff and the prince of Naples held him steady for the oak from the witch's crown to swallow pine, flesh, fire, and dark spirit all—pegged in its knotty entrails.

Resplendent in its victory, the young oak spirit shivered in pride at Miranda's gratitude. A boastful one, but all oaks were.

Arms too heavy to lower—her fingers entwined between foliage and the sky—Miranda made one last request of the old witch freed from Ariel's influence. Cal faded from Miranda's awareness, free of the sap that had bound them.

"Be free, and fare thee well," she whispered, spirit soft.

For him, the elements.

To the witches, the earth, and the growing, and the harvests.

Miranda, come...

Silver hands plucked her from the dirt and up towards the stars. Cal held her steady as she slipped through the air. He was warm, more substantial than starlight. Or she had grown cold and soft to match.

In the space between the rooted earth and the pinned sky, two spirits made of moon silver danced to a chorus of the four winds around an old willow with wood like bone and leaves like hair, a verdant oak and an elder that knelt at their feet, a bone shard erupting from a dead witch's heartwood until the slow drip of drying sap stopped, leaving only the sound of the winds, singing.

SUCH SWEET UNCLEANNESS
(MEASURE FOR MEASURE)
AMELIA MANGAN

The city had been built on filth. Deepest roots in muck and mire, foundations sunk in rotting vegetation and disintegrating bone. So much human effort had gone toward concealing the evidence; so much clean white paper and sticky red tape unwound by the yard; so much thick salt sweat and so much bruised flesh in the beating back of the swampland that had been here first, had always been here, would remain, buried under a million tons of concrete. Now, great spiraling towers of glass and steel sliced into neon night, bleeding electric glare across the sky. The city, which, like all great structures, longed to collapse back into the primordial dark, was kept staggering and exhausted on its feet beneath the weight of a hundred thousand burning lights.

Angelo stared at those lights from beneath a haze of swamp miasma, watching them sway and bob with the rhythm of the boat, and thought about how much it had cost to keep them on, every single one. He would know; he'd been on the committee to determine how much of the city's budget ought to be expended on electrical wiring, and it had been he who'd argued that it deserved a much greater chunk of that budget than it currently had. After all, he'd reminded his colleagues, the more illumination, the greater the visibility. Fewer dark corners for sin to breed; fewer shaded alleys and doorways where vice could reach fruition. With that blazing eye upon you at all times, who could find the nerve to fornicate? What man could look at his whore for the night and fail to see the lines of her face, the sag of her skin, the reflection of one's own bestial ugliness in her vacant eye?

The argument had been successful, as Angelo's arguments usually were. Back then, he'd been on a lot of committees. Infrastructure committee, Roads and Causeways committee, Health and Safety committee. He had understood that ensconcing oneself in as many committees as possible was a necessary step toward the ultimate goal of establishing sole authority, answerable to no committee at all. In this, too, he had been successful: SECRETARY FOR MORAL HYGIENE read the title stenciled in gold across his office door, and so what if the office itself was still cramped and small and lonesome? So what if it still faced a brick wall cobwebbed with cracks and interlaced with black dirt, a dirt Angelo found himself staring at more and more as the paperwork piled up and his responsibilities metastasized and the electrified nights blazed on into endless gray dawns? Gaining the title had been a triumph. The bill he had written to outlaw houses of prostitution had been a triumph. The follow-up bill, outlawing prostitution entirely—that was to say, any sexual union unblessed by marriage, as defined in a mildewed citywide law all the other cabinet members had been too lazy or stupid or personally debauched to unearth—had been a triumph. And when he looked up at the dull strip of fluorescent light above his head, when its unceasing hum penetrated into his brain and thrummed behind his eyeballs like the buzz of blood in a vein, he simply closed his eyes and counted that, too, as a triumph.

So much power was expended now, week after week, just to keep the lights on. To make sure they stayed bright and blazing and hard. But out here, drawing farther and farther away from the city, the lights' reflections in the brackish water were weak, shivering things—barely even guttering candles. Certainly not strong enough to see by. That was all right. Some things were better left in the dark.

He could hardly even see his own face anymore—knife-slash mouth, beetled brows, high white forehead streaked with lines of care. A striking man, some people called him, if they thought they could curry his favor. Sometimes, when circumstance forced him to creep outside his office, he would pass by women—sucking down black liquid at the coffee machine, typing with painted talons behind desks, waiting on stiletto heels by the elevators. When they looked at him, if they looked at all, he could sense their disdain, feel their swollen lips twitch with revulsion. If a clutch of them were standing together, they would erupt in cawing laughter, and even though they weren't looking his way, he knew they laughed at him.

I was almost married, he wanted to tell them, and reminded himself now. *I was so close. She wanted me. It was frightening how much she wanted me.*

He did not want to think of Mariana. He would not think of Mariana. Mariana had been a failure, and tonight was to be another triumph. Even if it didn't really feel that way just yet.

Angelo glanced at the boatman. Draped in a shrouding cowl, his callused hands entwined around a driftwood oar. The man had uttered not one word since his arrival at the dock, for which Angelo was grateful. What kind of conversation could they possibly have? The man was aware of Angelo's purpose. Isabella would have told him. If she valued herself, as Angelo knew she did, she would have instructed him to keep his silence.

Isabella.

Angelo saw his eyelids flutter, lashes striking the uppermost slant of his cheekbones, like a lovelorn girl. A throb of loathing tore through him at the sight—grotesque, under the circumstances. Under *any* circumstances. Better to think of this as a transaction, something that did not compromise the integrity of either one of them. And he respected her integrity, he truly did. They spoke the same language: he understood her, and in her high and rigid control he had felt, for the first time, that here was someone who understood him. He knew exactly how hard it was to stay taut and poised and ever watchful of oneself. To not allow oneself, ever, to fall apart.

Perhaps he'd sensed this, somehow, when the phone had rung and the security guard told him, in halting tones of apology, that there were women waiting for him down in the lobby: "A bunch of them, five in all, but, sir, they ain't just women."

"What are they, exactly?" Angelo had intoned, imbuing his voice with a boredom he did not quite feel.

"Well, sir, they're sisters."

"A family, then. So what?"

"No, sir. Like...*religious* sisters. The Sisterhood of the Marsh, they call themselves."

Angelo's mouth quirked. "The cult from way out in the swamp? They're beyond our jurisdiction."

"Maybe so, but one of 'em, their leader I think, she's got this brother, like a *real* brother, and he's in some kind of legal trouble and they say you can help him. His name's Claudio or something, don't know if that means anything to you."

Angelo tapped at his keyboard and watched as a mugshot materialized on his desktop screen. A thin, feral youth, barely eighteen, his long dark hair a wild scribble over hunted eyes.

The guard's voice dropped. "They're really kinda spooky, sir. Maybe you wanna send 'em away?"

"No," Angelo said. "Send them up."

He drew the blinds of his office, perched on the back of his couch and peered between the shadowed slats as the elevator doors slid apart and in they floated, in they *swept*. Five of them, as the guard had said, and all in midnight blue. Layers of torn lace and shredded velvet, draped over lowered heads, sliding soundless over marble, drifting past cubicles and desks like anemones in deep-sea tides. Angelo saw that one of them—the tallest, standing in the center of the phalanx, armored by her companions' bodies—did not walk with her head down; she was staring past her veil, past the window and the blinds, at him.

Angelo sprang back and propelled himself behind his desk, where he steepled his fingers and tried to still his heart.

A mistake, he thought. *An error. You should never have allowed that one up here. The others, maybe. Not that one.*

Knuckles rapped his door, only once. He could tell from the location of the knock that it was one of the smaller ones. Of course. *That* one would not do her own knocking.

"Enter," he called. "*One* of you."

SUCH SWEET UNCLEANNESS

A hesitation. This had thrown them. Angelo smiled.

The doorknob rolled. The golden letters of his name caught the omnipresent light as the door inched inwards.

Her smell. Not a scent, not a perfume, nothing so delicate as that. A *smell*. It preceded her into the room. Filled the space from corner to corner, inescapable. Animal, ordure, and earth. Sodden mud beneath leather boots. Wet fur. Dust on leaves. The sweet violet of rotting meat.

The smell filled Angelo's nasal cavity, slid down the back of his throat. He tasted it on his tongue. He wanted to retch, to purge his system of this poison. He wanted to bury his face in a pool of it and drink until he drowned.

He had not seen her move into the room. His eyes were watering, salt-stung. Now here she stood before his desk, straight as a sword. Directly under the light, and yet the fluorescent glare only seemed to throw her into deeper shade beneath her veil; if he looked closely (and he knew he should not look closely, should not look at all), he could just make out, against that shadowed mesh, the swell of lip, the curve of jaw, the delicate latticework of blinking lash.

Angelo forced his vocal cords into motion and asked, in as flat and dead a tone as he could muster, "Won't you sit down, Miss—?"

"Isabella," she said. Her voice. A rush of cold wind over black water. "We prefer to stand."

Angelo shuffled some papers on his desk, just for something to do. "Would that be 'Sister' Isabella?"

"Reverend Mother Isabella," she said. "Only our brother calls us sister."

"Mm," said Angelo. "Well, not for very much longer."

The blow landed. He saw a flicker behind the veil, black lightning, and smiled as placidly as he knew how. "I really do think you should sit."

She sat. Ran her hands up the leather arms, wrapped clawed fingers around the ends. A line of moisture followed the path of her hands, like the trail of a slug. Angelo would have to have the cleaners in after she left. Get the chair sanitized. *Or you could just lick it clean yourself,* he thought, and dug his nails into the back of his hand to chase the thought away.

"You are familiar with the case we plead," Isabella said. Nothing in her tone suggested either a question or pleading.

"I am, yes." Angelo leafed meaninglessly through his papers. "Claudio, isn't it? Your younger brother. Did you know, Reverend Mother, that he is one of the very first offenders jailed under this city's Secondary-Prostitution Act?" He shook his head. "And only just turned eighteen. Tragic. But—" He shrugged, helpless. "The law is the law."

"Out in the swamp, we have laws of our own," said Isabella. "Kindly restore our brother to us, and we will deal with Claudio accordingly."

"My understanding is that Claudio's accomplice in the act fled the scene," Angelo said, "and is already in your custody."

"Juliet. Yes. She is with us."

"Indeed. And how have you dealt with *her*?"

"We will determine that later. She is with child."

"Ah." Angelo sat back, tapping at his lower lip. "Well. I'm saddened to hear that, Reverend Mother. Deeply saddened. To think that a man, even a young and feckless one, would compound his own disgrace by inflicting a bastard child on the girl he lured into corruption." He sighed. "What a shame."

"The child is no 'bastard'," Isabella said, and Angelo heard the click of her teeth as she bit off the word. "Claudio and Juliet are married."

Angelo raised his eyebrows. "Married?"

"Yes."

"Under *our* law?"

The high proud head dipped, ever so slightly. The blue filigree at the edge of her veil brushed the rounded tops of her thighs. "Under swamp law," she said. Her voice was satisfyingly muted.

"I see," said Angelo. He leaned back in his chair. "Well, I'm sorry, Reverend Mother. There's simply nothing I can do for you. You can file a petition at the courthouse, but, if I'm honest, I don't imagine it'll do much good. My advice is simply to lend Claudio as much support as you can—he'll need it, he must be terribly scared—and try to accept the inevitable." He stood, gesturing toward the door. "My secretary can give you a list of counseling services for those similarly bereaved, and of course, any legal advice my office can provide—"

"We were told you were a man of character," Isabella said, making no move to get up. "A man of conviction."

Angelo coughed up a laugh as he moved to her side. "What I am, Reverend Mother, is a man with an inordinate amount of work to do, and I'm afraid I *really* don't have any more time—"

She turned her eyes up to him, then, and he could see them wet and wide and dark through the fabric, and his stomach roiled and clenched and he knew, with the certainty of desperation, that if she did not leave, if she did not leave his office and get in the elevator and head back out to the swamp *right now*, he would be lost forever.

She reached out from beneath the slashed lace of her veil. Her damp, cool hand clasped his. It was over.

"Tell me," she said. "Are you a man who has loved?"

Angelo's voice, when it came, was as limp as his hand. "I had a fiancée."

"Had. What became of her?"

"She drowned."

"Then you know." Her thumbnail dug into his palm, a bright sharp thorn. "You know the feel of cold wood beneath your knees in the frozen moments of the dawn. You know the rough chafe of one hand pressed so hard into the other your lifelines bleed into one. You know the hoarse mutterings of your own voice, unfamiliar to your ear, offering bargains you'd never imagined to gods you cannot see. You must know."

Angelo, who knew none of these things, slid his hand from hers and sat back down behind his desk. A fine sweat dusted his shoulder blades, and he could see spots behind his eyes each time he blinked. He crossed his legs, trying to tamp down the raging beast between them, harder and hungrier than he'd ever known it to be.

The blinds were still down. Fortunate that he had thought to close them. Or perhaps he'd known—ever since he'd laid eyes on her, ever since he'd told the guard to bring her up—what was going to happen.

"You mentioned bargains," he said, and felt his heavy tongue swipe parched lips. "Tell me of them."

Isabella inclined her head. "There is little in this life that we would not give up for our brother," she said. "Little we would not promise."

"And these promises," Angelo said. "You keep them? Always?"

"The Sisterhood's word is as true as its heart."

"I don't believe the Sisterhood has anything to offer me."

The draped shoulders sagged. A motion of despair, defeat. Angelo's entire body pulsated at the sight.

"Very well. We must go to comfort our brother, sir. Thank you for your—"

"I believe *you* have something to offer me."

Her back straightened. She looked at him again, and though he could not see her eyes this time, he felt them questing across the numb terrain of his face, over the hollow cheeks into which his molars bit, to the lips he'd set in a line to keep from trembling.

This isn't my fault, he thought. *Anything that happens now. You can't blame me. If you hadn't been what you are. If you hadn't come to me, thinking I was the kind of man who would never do something like this. If you hadn't placed yourself at my feet, I would never have wanted you on your knees.*

"We don't believe we understand," said Isabella, in a voice so cold and clear, it was apparent she understood completely.

"I think we'd both rather I didn't have to say it aloud," said Angelo.

Isabella rose, slowly, and leaned across the desk. Her veil pooled in folds on the tabletop, spilling over into Angelo's lap. "You would dare?" she hissed. "You would *dare* importune us in such a manner?"

Angelo stared back at her, gaze-level. The inside of his mouth was completely dry. "Think of it as a formal agreement," he said. "A fair exchange. This doesn't have to be sordid, you know. Not unless you make it that way."

"Our brother's head for our body," Isabella said. The veil rippled as she let out a huffed, sneering breath. "This you consider a 'fair exchange'?"

"Don't you?"

"Better a thousand brothers die than we surrender our chastity."

"Just the one will have to do," said Angelo.

Isabella drew back. "This will not stand," she said, voice low. "We will raise hue and cry. We will tell all. We will make it our mission to ruin you."

"Go ahead," Angelo said, as blandly as he could. "I've spent years building a reputation in this city. Rallied a good deal of support. The Mayor trusts me implicitly, and if the polls are right, the voting public seems to, as well. You said it yourself: people say I'm a man of character. Of conviction. They *know* me."

He stood, moved around the desk, and came before her under the buzzing light. Their foreheads almost touched. He could feel her breath. "And *you*," he whispered, "don't know anybody at all."

He marveled at the memory, even now, as the boatman rowed deeper into the swamplands and the moon, as if in shame, disappeared in a tumble of black clouds. That he—Angelo, who believed in rule and law, who respected chastity and virtue, who had only ever made a mistake once before, only the once—could actually have uttered such words, felt them deep in his marrow and his sex. He'd read about men like him, other politicians and bureaucrats who'd laid waste to their own lives for the sake of a gasp and a spasm; he'd laughed about it to himself, wondering how in the world any man could possibly be so stupid, so absolutely wayward and lost.

But when Isabella had stared back at him, when he'd felt her blink, when he'd heard her grind out those two blessed, accursed words: *"All right"*—at last, he'd understood.

"I ask one thing," she said, in that same delicious whipped-dog tone, as she went to leave.

"Certainly," Angelo said, feeling like a magnanimous king.

"You will not speak."

"Of course," said Angelo. "I won't tell a soul." He paused. "I know it's hard for you to understand, Isabella, but truly, I have no desire to cause you— "

"You will not *speak*," Isabella went on, as if he had not spoken now, "when you come to me. Not before the deed. Not during. Not when it is done. Do you find these terms acceptable?"

That last part had sounded vaguely sarcastic, but he decided to let it go. "I do."

"Good." Brisk, clipped. Businesslike. She was recovering, then.

Already adjusting to the idea. Angelo suppressed a brief stab of disappointment.

"The dock at midnight, then. When the moon wanes. The boatman will collect you."

"The dock?" Angelo said, thinking of all the lights he'd had turned on, the city's endless and pitiless illumination. "But what if I'm seen?"

He could not be certain, but he thought he sensed her smile. It was a sharp, serrated thing.

"You will be well hidden," she said. "The dark provides for its own."

Angelo reached out and trailed a hand through the water, shredding his reflection to glassy ribbons. She had been right. No one had noticed him. He might have been a phantom. *A vampire*, he thought. Wending its way toward its latest victim, on silent and determined leather wings.

The sluggish black vein of the river narrowed, twisted to a bend. Soft green phosphorescence glimmered on mudslide banks; bright, inhuman eyes darted between emaciated trees. Sleeping birds chittered in the ivy and bullfrogs splashed quietly in the shallows, yet Angelo saw nothing that breathed. A mosquito whined in his ear. He slapped it against his neck, and when he drew his hand back, saw that it was bloody.

The boy would still have to die, of course. There had never really been any question about that. If such degeneracy were overlooked, it would set precedent, and open the door for a thousand appeals. People would wonder how Angelo, virtue's fiercest champion, could possibly have been moved to defend an act he had previously deemed indefensible. There would be questions, speculation, rumor. Unprovable, obviously. But unacceptable.

More importantly, if the boy's sentence went ahead as planned, that would mean what was to occur tonight would never really have occurred at all. In a way, Angelo thought, he wasn't even here right now. Just as it hadn't been him saying those things in his office; just as it hadn't been him with Mariana (*not Mariana, don't think of Mariana*). Deeds could be erased, time turned backward, tarnished souls burnished bright as silver. Sometimes things just didn't happen, even if they did.

Another bend in the river, and a tawny glow appeared up ahead, along with the thick scent of burning cypress. Angelo squinted against the smoke and, as the boat bumped softly against the bank, he saw a long stretch of unkempt grass flattened by the reeking air. On it, a vast and roaring bonfire. A lone silhouette kneeled before it, three small rough hillocks placed equidistant all around. Beyond the grassland, cloaked in trees on either side and falling away into black water behind, an unpainted one-room shack stood tall and imperious on rough-hewn stilts, raised above the murk of the swamp.

Angelo willed himself steady as he straightened. His trembling hand shook the side of the boat as he clambered out; he almost apologized to the boatman, but thought better of it. The man was already steering away, as wordless and implacable as he'd ever been, and anyway, it was pointless to apologize for anything now.

He took a breath, wrapped his coat tight around himself, and began to cross the clearing. As he drew closer to the heat and fury of the bonfire, he saw that the kneeling figure was a girl, hair a red tangle, her skinny body unshielded from the night air in a diaphanous white nightgown. She held a wooden box in her lap as she gazed into the flames. The three lumpen shapes surrounding her were slumbering boars, their red tongues laid on beds of yellow teeth, with unseeing eyes gleaming white.

Angelo tried not to look. The girl's head snapped to one side as he moved through the grass, and she watched him pass with sullen, red-lined eyes. The rounded swell of her belly drew the thin material of her nightgown taut against her skin.

As he approached the house and the opposing shore beyond, the ground beneath his feet grew waterlogged and malleable. It sucked at his shoes, a gravitational force demanding he give in, render unto the swamp that which was the swamp's. Angelo could feel it in the secret hollows of the body, the empty core of the bone: that animal need to buckle and bend, to be swept under, closed off from desire and fear. *This is what we fight against*, he thought. *This feeling, in this place. This is where all control comes to drown.*

A shelf of uneven steps led up to the shadowed enclosure of the porch. The curtains, dark blue, were drawn, and no light emerged from beneath them. Angelo wondered if perhaps Isabella had elected not to come. He could understand that. He could turn around himself, right now, and leave this place. But he knew she was here. She lingered. He could taste the air she breathed.

The door was unlocked, and as it swung open he saw nothing within. Perfect dark.

He took one step, another. Past the threshold now. *Close the door*, he thought, *and there'll be no returning. All choices will have been made.*

He closed the door.

A wash of blindness. Warm and dark as the inside of an eyelid. Angelo raised a hand, and moved the fingers inches from his face. He felt the motion, the minute working of muscles, but saw no hand before him. *Not here*, he thought. *You're not truly here after all.*

Thin outlines came to him, more like visions in a dream than the adjustment of an eye. Neat black floorboard furrows. Triangulated corners, and the high, arched back of an armchair beneath the furthest one. Hard black bars and pale draperies, torn white ghosts of gossamer, and he realized he was looking upon a great canopied brass bed.

"Welcome," said Isabella.

Close and deep, inside his eardrum. She was here, seated within the armchair, a web of cracked leather at her back. Her veil remained down, but her robes had ridden—been raised?—all the way up, past knees, over thighs, almost to her sex. High black boots, polished to a brilliant shine, were planted wide apart on the wood. A stick was laid across her knees, almost a staff, and though her clawed hands grasped each end with a relaxed firmness, Angelo saw no blade or sharpened point, nothing that would indicate threat.

"Remember your promise," she said, as his lips parted.

Angelo remembered, and closed his mouth. He wondered if he ought to take off his coat. The room was so warm, and her smell so thick in the close darkness: a sticky and viscous thing, seeping, malodorous, more secretion than scent. It dizzied him like smoke from a censer, churning in his guts like bad milk. He was so hard it hurt.

"Lay down," her voice commanded.

He obeyed. The draperies snatched at his limbs, twisted and tore.

The bed was unyielding, but a soft white pillow had been propped up at its head. He moved to lay it flat.

"No," Isabella said. "Keep your head up." He heard something in her voice now, a breath, a smile. "You can see in the dark now. And we *want* you to see."

Angelo felt his mouth flood with saliva, and he swallowed it down. Her thighs were slabs of bloodless meat. No light had ever touched that flesh—not the sun, not the moon, and, most of all, not the blinking neon, the buzzing fluorescent strip. She was a hidden thing. No one had ever truly seen her. Only he ever would.

Angelo shucked his coat, threw it to one side, and lay back on the bed.

"We wonder, Angelo," said Isabella, "what prompts a man to reject the night. What calls him to burn it away from the inside out, incinerate it on an electrical grid, chase every shadow from every corner. Perhaps it is because he considers this his duty. Perhaps it is because he fears what he cannot see, that which can only be touched to be known. Or—" Her voice flowed from the chair to the foot of the bed "—perhaps it is because he already knows what awaits him there."

The door opened. The red-haired girl slid inside on a thread of moonlight. The door closed and the thread snapped, but not before Angelo glimpsed the box in her arms. He thought of protesting her presence—it was Isabella he had come for, and he wanted her bare and quiet and all alone, all to himself—but the smell was too strong now, a tightening noose around his neck.

The girl handed Isabella the box and stalked around the bed, eyeing Angelo with indifferent appetite. She sat down in the vacated armchair and curled up, head on one hand.

"If you want to know what *we* believe, Angelo," said Isabella, and he heard her staff rap the floorboards as she propped it against the bedstead. "What *I* believe. I do not believe we obey duty because it is right and proper. I believe that every duty is created to allay a fear, and that behind every fear lurks a craving."

She opened the box, and drew out Claudio's head.

Angelo saw himself bolting upright. He imagined what he would sound like, crying out. He felt the floorboards thundering under his heels as he ran from this place, this woman.

He remained prone. Voiceless.

"Perhaps, after all," Isabella said, looking into her brother's frosted eyes, "this was what *I* craved."

She gripped the head by the hair, touched a tender hand to the unshaven cheek. "Do I not have my freedom now? None can hold power over me. None can wield my love as a dangling sword above my head. What tie exists to bind me? I am released."

She thrust the sliced trunk of the neck down upon the tip of the staff until the wood bulged the throat, until the ghastly sketch of white on black seemed to hover of its own accord, an apparition, watching over the bed.

Angelo's hands were withered things, boneless at his sides, and his legs were as cordwood. *You should fight*, he thought. *Spring from this bed, knock her to the ground. Beat her brains in against the floor. Strangle the whelp in the chair, for good measure.*

But there was something else, beyond thought. A growing sense in him, curious and wondrous and awful, that this was all entirely correct. All things were proceeding exactly as they should.

"Even *he* would have had me in a snare," Isabella said, inclining her head toward her brother's. "When I spoke with him, after speaking with you, he approved your terms. He valued his life more than his sister's honor. He believed I should feel the same. After all, did I not love him?"

She circled the staff, a slow half-moon. "I confess: in that moment, I felt I did not. I felt that my love for him had died. I willed it to die. Ah, but that's the hard thing about love, isn't it, Angelo? Like justice, it never really dies. Only waits. Sleeping. You have been here before."

Angelo waited. No point hoping she didn't know, no point in denial or pretense. He understood what was coming.

"Out here. To the swamplands." She came to the head of the bed and knelt, her head on the pillow beside his. The veil was wet. Her eyes were pools of black compassion. "The fear, Angelo. All these years. The fear must have been so great. The craving behind it so dreadful. You have been sleeping, too, all this time, with the lights on."

Her love, Angelo thought. *Oh, Mariana. Her love was so vast.*

She hadn't been a rich woman. Not what he'd needed, oh no. Not a society woman, not poised and refined, trained for her role. Not at all the kind of woman a man like him, with ambitions like his, would ever truly marry. She had nothing to her name, nothing at all. Only a love as deep and wide and lightless as all the oceans of all the world. Neither league nor fathom could measure it. You could always feel its pull, its riptide current dragging you under.

"It wasn't *her* you brought out here, Angelo. Not really." *Was that Isabella? Was she speaking? Had she ever stopped?* There must be a point where his thoughts ended and her speech began, but the line dividing them had been cut, perhaps had never been there to begin with. "Wasn't *her* you pulled down and held under, until the heartbeat ceased. You know that. It was your need. Your helplessness. Your craving to close your eyes and fall into the dark."

You wanted to drown in her, thought Angelo. *In a woman. Any woman. Every woman. It was always there, in you, from the very beginning. You had to do something. You had to save yourself.*

A shadow, kinked and broken, rose up from behind the armchair. The red-haired girl stroked her belly, as if to calm what lay inside.

Isabella turned her head to watch the shadow grow, to watch as it threw spider-limbed echoes of itself across the dusty floor, and as hands gloved in loose wet tatters of skin grasped at the cracks in the boards, dug splinter-deep into the wood. Angelo watched with her. Something inside, something greater than himself that he had never allowed full reign, observed that he was feeling fear—yes, a terrible, anesthetizing fear—but this greater, wiser part of himself knew now that the fear was only a mask after all, only a veil. The small, weak light left on to comfort the fretting child at bedtime. Once that light went out, one could finally begin to see.

"The struggle is over," said Isabella. He felt her drawing away. "The fear has passed. All you have craved, you shall have. Rejoice, Angelo! Receive Isabella's blessing. Be sated, and be happy, and know Mariana still loves you."

A sodden knee on one side of the bed, and another thrown across his hips. A smell of mud clawed up from the bottom of the river, blood and clay, the black oil of dead prehistoric monsters. The slick greasy drip of sex and stagnant water.

Knotted whips of black hair stuck to his lips. He swallowed the strands, took them into himself. His hands, which he had not known could move and had never moved this way, were on her hips, around her back, spreading the nested lips between her legs; and now inside, under the flayed skin, stroking raw muscle, tracing each exquisite nerve to its end. He sucked at the honeyed sickness of her mouth.

As she enfolded him, all around, he could feel his body starting to come apart. His flesh, so rigid and clean for so long, was turning to hot and molten filth. Each mote and molecule was on the move, dissembling, dissolving. Exhaling into the collapse.

His arms were sinking into her. Long strings of liquid skin bound his legs to hers. They *were* the swamp now, he and Mariana: formless channels of sluicing meat, tributaries flowing one into the other.

They were coming together. He was falling apart. He had never known such joy.

At last, he knew no more. There was no more to know.

A lump of melted flesh, which had once been man and woman, writhed slowly beneath a bridal canopy on a heavy brass bed. A young girl watched with half-lidded eyes, languid fingers tracing her stretch marks. A bird sang, somewhere deep in the swamp. All was soft, and wet, and dark.

THE MARRIAGE OF BEATRICE MESSINA

(MUCH ADO ABOUT NOTHING)

EMMA SELLE

The family sat in the front room, quiet and subdued. A heavy rain beat at the windows and an eerie wind howled, rattling the windowpanes and whistling throughout the house. Leonato and Antonio sat at the desk in the corner, poring over documents and murmuring. Hero, Ursula, and Margaret sat on the sofa; one wrote in her diary, another stabbed at her needlework, and the last sipped a lukewarm cup of tea from the morning's breakfast. Beatrice sat a little apart, absorbed in a book of verse and idly wrapping and unwrapping a lock of hair around her forefinger.

Hero pulled her shawl more tightly against her shoulders after the motion of writing caused it to slip. Ursula wished the tea was still hot. Margaret felt dreary as she stabbed her needle through the linen again and again, staring out at the oppressive gray of clouds that hung low over the winter-barren fields. She hissed in pain when she pricked her finger; a dark spot of blood marred her needlework. Beatrice looked up and twisted her lips sympathetically as Margaret stuck the wounded finger in her mouth, frowning.

A loud knocking at the door disrupted the stillness of the sitting room. Everyone jumped, heads snapping toward the door. Margaret pricked another finger and muttered an oath, setting down her embroidery. Leonato stood as the footman entered, escorting a drenched messenger who stayed at the edge of the rug, dripping rainwater onto the stone floor.

"A letter of importance for Your Grace." He handed a missive to the footman, who bore it over the swathe of blue carpet to Leonato's outstretched hand.

All eyes trained on the Duke as he broke the seal, unfolded the letter, and read it quickly. "Is this correct?" he asked, looking up to address the messenger, handing the letter to Antonio. "Don Pedro and his company approach, seeking refuge?"

"Indeed. I hardly outpaced them; my lord ought to arrive by nightfall."

"He is welcome," Leonato said. "How do he and his men fare?"

The messenger's expression tightened. "Victorious, though it was hard-won. Few of name were lost but many wounded. It is largely thanks to the valiant young Claudio that they emerged victorious. Don Pedro has recognized Claudio's bravery and hopes, with your aid and hospitality, to continue to show him true thanks."

"Celebrations will be well in order."

"Please," said Beatrice, rising from her seat, a finger among the book's pages to keep her place. "Do you have any news of Sir Valiant? He is in Don Pedro's company."

The messenger looked at her, befuddled. "I do not know who you mean, lady."

Hero raised a brow at Beatrice. "My cousin means Sir Benedick. She loves to challenge his wits to battle whenever he returns from battles of sterner stuff. She struggles to know when to be serious."

Beatrice smiled. "A true accusation, I fear. I will put it more plainly: is there any news of Sir Benedick to relay? He was close with Don Pedro, but he is always turning a new leaf and adopting a new bosom-friend to hang on like a disease until they weary of him. So, has Don Pedro shaken him yet? Or does Benedick near this house with the company?" Beatrice's eyes shone with unspoken laughter and so it took her a moment to notice the tension that seized the room. The messenger stood, frozen, his face screwed up in an uncomfortable grimace. "Sir?"

"My lady," the messenger spoke haltingly, "I bear sad news. Sir Benedick fought at young Claudio's side and died on the field. He is mourned by the whole company."

All eyes turned to Beatrice, who felt suddenly lightheaded. Her book slipped from her hands, falling upon the rug with a soft thump. She pressed a hand to her stomach to steady herself. Hero crossed the room to take her elbow.

"Please, forgive my daughter," Antonio said to the messenger. "She did not intend to be callous; it is just that she and Benedick have—*had* an ongoing battle of jests, which she continues whenever possible. Had she known—"

"I would never have spoken so," Beatrice said breathlessly. She lifted her eyes, vacant now of laughter. "Please give my sincere condolences to all whom he leaves behind. He—" Her voice broke and she sat heavily, pale and drawn.

"I will take my cousin to retire," Hero said, helping Beatrice to her feet and winding an arm about her waist. "Thank you, sir, for bearing the burden of your news. We will prepare to welcome the rest of the regiment."

Quickly and quietly, the other ladies flocked about Beatrice, picking up her book and bearing her out of the room and into Hero's antechamber. They turned up the lamps and wrapped a warm wool throw about Beatrice, who stared vacantly at the lamp's flame.

Hero quietly bade Margaret and Ursula go before she sat across from Beatrice and gently took her hand, squeezing her cold, pale fingers. "Beatrice?" she said softly. "You seem suddenly ill."

"I think I am," she whispered. "A deep, yawning pit seems to have opened in my chest, Hero. It vexes me as much as it hurts me, for I never before realized—" Her voice tightened and a tear rolled heavily down her cheek.

Hero nodded. "You loved Benedick."

The tears fell in earnest as Beatrice nodded, and then she crumpled, burying her head in her cousin's dress as she wept. "I learned it too late," she cried.

Hero said nothing, only stroking Beatrice's hair.

By supper, Beatrice had recovered herself enough to sit at the table. The heavy burgundy brocade curtains were pulled tightly shut against the night. Every candle had been lit, suffusing the room with flickering golden light that played at the shadows in the corners. Beatrice passed her time by studying the dimly lit faces and bright conversations filling the hall. Her confused grief still stole the fire from her eyes and from her tongue, but it mattered little; supper was late, having awaited the arrival of the regiment. So great was the men's merriment at a warm welcome and hot, hearty fare that they hardly noticed one silent girl and her pale face.

Well, hardly anyone. Hero glanced over in concern throughout the evening, though her looks grew fewer and fewer as the night wore on. She was seated beside the young Claudio, who was fair of face and temper. Though reserved at first, he was soon easily conversing with the equally young and fair Hero. Beatrice marked their smiling exchanges and her cousin's lessening ministrations but found herself unperturbed at being unattended. Hero deserved every happiness, and Beatrice would be quite all right in time.

Something flickered at the corner of her eye. Frowning, Beatrice turned to look. Her eyes fell upon Don Pedro, who was caught in conversation with her father. When the pair looked over at her—Antonio's face lined with concern and Don Pedro's with thoughtfulness—Beatrice quickly looked away.

But there, again; a flicker! A slight shimmer, like heat rising off a flame. Beatrice almost smiled at her own foolishness. A candle's flame wavered just before her eyes, in the very space where she thought something had flitted. It was merely her overwrought emotions rendering her foolish. She closed her eyes momentarily before standing and walking to Leonato.

"I am sorry, uncle, but I shall have to retire for the evening," she said quietly, not wishing to disrupt the festivities.

Leonato turned and took her hand, gently squeezing it with understanding. "I shall see you in the morning, my dear niece," he said.

Beatrice smiled and ignored the eyes that followed her as she left.

The corridors were long and dark, eerily quiet after the cheerful clamor of the dining room. It still stormed outside, and a cold draft curled about her ankles as she walked. A shiver ran down her back, lifting the hair on her neck.

Turning the corner toward her room, Beatrice found it entirely dark save a candelabra at the end of the hall. Frowning, she withdrew a few paces and claimed a candle from another sconce. Protecting the guttering flame with her hand, she began down the dark corridor.

As she neared her door, a gust of cold air fluttered through her hair and rustled her skirts. It blew out not only the candle she held, but also the flames at the end of the hall. Plunged into darkness, a spillage of wax fell onto the back of her hand. As it cooled and solidified, a bone-deep cold suddenly engulfed Beatrice where she stood.

Beatrice froze, blinking in the immediate blackness. Her door was only steps away, but quickening fear held her fast. Her breathing shallowed and she felt certain someone was there in the dark, though she had thought herself alone.

Straightening her spine and lowering the useless, cold candlestick, Beatrice spoke into the abysmal darkness, her breath clouding the wintry air. "I am going to bed. I will not be disturbed. Any matters of importance can be taken downstairs to my father and uncle or they may wait until morning."

Deeply unsettled and stiff with cold, Beatrice forced her numb legs into motion, groping her way to her door, wallpaper rasping beneath her fingertips. The cold metal of the door handle bit into Beatrice's palm. She gasped at the shock but nevertheless quickly pushed it open before locking it behind. She leaned against the solid door as her fingers regained feeling and her heart slowed its frantic beating.

She looked about her familiar, comfortable room, warmly lit with lamps and the bed turned invitingly down. She felt quite foolish. There had been no one in the hall. A draft had blown out the candles; stormy cold had plagued the house all day. She was only distraught, imagining phantoms in the night.

Beatrice readied herself for bed and fell quickly into a fitful slumber, though she left a lamp burning low.

That Saturday was a masquerade ball, celebrating the valiant return of the brave regiment. Even the rain stopped for the occasion, though dark clouds still hung low and threatening over the hills. The household bustled with preparation. Hero swooned over Claudio. Yet Beatrice could not shake her sadness over Benedick.

In the evening, after the public began to arrive, everyone hurried downstairs. For their grand entrance, Leonato and Hero, the hosts, would enter first. Don Pedro, honored guest, would follow. That left Antonio and Beatrice the last in line.

Antonio took his daughter's hand, placing it on his arm. As the doors were heaved open, he asked, "How do you fare? You look a bit better this evening."

Beatrice smiled. "I am well enough, Father. I will be all aright soon. It is merely a passing ailment of my humor."

Antonio patted her hand. "I hope to see you married and happy. Sir Benedick would have been a worthy suitor. I am sorry that such a match cannot be."

Beatrice concealed the twist of her heart with a brittle laugh. "When he lived, I thought Benedick thoroughly below my interest, and have only thought better of it too late. I think, perhaps, God made me for loneliness. But worry not," she said, seeing the concern on her father's face and smiling more truthfully, "I find freedom in loneliness. I was happy as ever when I thought love was far from my heart; I will be happy again when the loss of it passes."

Antonio had no time to reply, for they were being announced. The pair donned their glittering masks and strode through the doors. At the foot of the grand staircase, the room surged as the music swelled and the dancing was opened by Hero and Don Pedro. Beatrice wove her way through the whirling crowd to find a chair. Once she did, she withdrew her fan from her reticule, beating it against the body-warmed air and watching the dancers twirl. It had been a long while since the last soiree, and the people of Messina had turned out in marvelous fashion. Rich colors swirled and gorgeous masks glittered.

THE MARRIAGE OF BEATRICE MESSINA

Peals of delighted chatter and happy laughter swirled with the music throughout the crowded ballroom.

Beatrice smiled at the display and almost wished to join them.

As though conjured by her thoughts, a man appeared before her. Beatrice blinked at the suddenness of his arrival. Much as several other men present, he wore a military uniform. His mask was a plain black shell over his face, dark hair peeking overtop, hair that—with a sudden painful twist—reminded her of Benedick.

He spoke in a warm voice that sounded like laughter. "Lady Disdain, why do you scorn the dance floor? Can no partner tempt you?"

Beatrice's eyes snapped to his in surprise. "Lady Disdain?" she repeated, standing. "Where have you heard that?"

"We can discuss it upon the dance floor," the suitor goaded, eyes glittering with humor, extending a hand.

"Very well," Beatrice said. "And I do not disdain the dance; I am simply aloof. And, you see, it worked: I attracted you."

The masked suitor laughed. Beatrice accepted his hand and noticed it was cold, even through their gloves. She frowned but covered the expression quickly.

"I count myself lucky." He led her to the edge of the dancers. Hand on her waist, he pulled her close. Beatrice's breath caught in her throat as he guided her fluidly through a waltz.

When he released her, the pair circling one another, she found her voice. "Have we met? Who is beneath the mask?"

The soldier pulled her close again. "I will not say. Why spoil the masquerade?"

"We must have met. We at least share a friend."

"Oh? Why do you say that?"

"'Lady Disdain.' Sir Benedick called me that; a joke between us. Though perhaps it wasn't for him." A bittersweet smile twisted her lips. "You are from his regiment; you must have known him."

The soldier shook his head. "Not particularly."

"Really?" Beatrice peered up into the masked face. "He died at Claudio's side. You never met?"

"What sort of man was he?"

Beatrice smiled. "Don Pedro's jester as much as his friend. His tongue flew faster than his wits. He was handsome and brave but quick to boast of both. He was well-loved by many and scorned by an equal number, for he never knew when to keep quiet. He could make someone wish him dead in one breath and laugh in the next. He was thoroughly imperfect."

"I see," the masked soldier said, amusement coloring his tone. "We may have met a time or two. What would he think if only he could hear how you speak of him tonight?"

"Oh, he would but make mocking comparisons to my own character. It was our game, trading insults. He always grew melancholy if he could get neither the last word nor laugh." Beatrice smiled again.

"I am sure you made the game a difficult one to win."

"I certainly got the last laugh," Beatrice said, her smile fading. "Though I am no merrier for it."

The music waned and there was a tap at Beatrice's shoulder. She turned to see Antonio, face drawn with concern. Hoping an introduction would win her the masked soldier's name, Beatrice turned back to him, only to find the space before her empty.

Suddenly, she noticed the gazes of all nearby dancers were trained on her, looking on with baffled disquiet.

"Let us go out for some air." Taking her arm, Antonio led her swiftly through the crowd and out of the ballroom. In the early spring chill of the garden below, Don Pedro, Leonato, and Hero were speaking quietly among the still-skeletal rose bushes. Their quiet conversation drifted past the tightly closed green buds that would not bloom for several weeks yet

In a dim corner of the terrace, Antonio drew to a stop. "Beatrice," he said seriously. "Why did you dance alone in such a manner? Are you still unwell? Need you to retire?"

Bewildered, Beatrice looked at her father. "I was not alone," she said slowly. "I danced with a soldier. Masked, much like the rest of us. I did not know him, but—"

"You danced with no one." Antonio gripped her shoulders, looking seriously into her face. "Naught but the air for a partner. It stalled the dancers around you. Do you jest, or did you truly imagine someone there?"

Beatrice paled at the earnestness in her father's eyes and the memory of the stricken dancers around her. Quickly, she twitched the corners of her lips into a reassuring smile. "I danced with memories, I suppose. I ought to have stayed to the side, to keep from disturbing the others. I am well, Father. Do not worry overmuch."

Antonio appeared unconvinced, but said, "I must go fetch Claudio. Stay here awhile and take the air?" With an affectionate pat to Beatrice's cheek, Antonio disappeared back into the cheery, warm ballroom.

Beatrice slowly sat on the low wall of the terrace. The masked soldier, who had reminded her so of Benedick...imagined? It could not be so. He had been so solid beneath her hands. She had felt him, noticed how cold he was. They had conversed. But the reaction of so many people could not be a fabrication. Was melancholy driving her to madness?

Her father reappeared with Claudio and went down into the garden. Don Pedro spoke to all of them briefly before leaving. Beatrice watched her father stand unobtrusively at her uncle's shoulder, facing Claudio and Hero. Claudio said something and a sunny smile lit Hero's face.

Don Pedro lowered himself to sit beside Beatrice, also looking down into the garden. "Are you well, fair Beatrice?" he asked.

"Indeed, I have a merry heart, if I perceive what is taking place rightly," she replied. "Claudio and Hero are to be wed?"

"With the blessings of all present," Don Pedro said. "They find themselves quite in love. I wish all happiness for them."

"Yes, a happy alliance. I am joyful for them, even if my place in the world is to sit in my lonely corner, watching as happy marriage passes me by." Beatrice's tone was playful and her joy for Hero true, but she felt a wan melancholy beneath it all.

"You may have as happy an alliance," Don Pedro said, his tone solemn.

"One of your careful choosing, my lord?" Beatrice joked.

"Mine and your father's," he answered, not joking.

Beatrice's smile faded as she weighed Don Pedro's words. She made one last halfhearted attempt at a jest. "Do you have a brother quite similar to you?"

He smiled. "You are a merry lady. Even in your sorrow, you cannot be serious. You must have been born in a laughing hour."

"Not at all. My mother cried, but above me, a star danced. So I am never sad for long."

"You would have been a right match for Benedick," Don Pedro said sadly. "You both loved to laugh, be it in joy or mockery. I wish your marriage could have been. In his absence, though, your father and I have spoken. My term of service ends soon. I am in want of a wife and your father worries for you. I am no Benedick; my tongue is not as fast, nor my wit as sharp. However, I am happy to bestow on you what I do have: my name, my fortune, my care. Will you have me, lady?"

Beatrice sat a moment in silent shock before she recovered her wits. "I am a poor lady to wear such a costly husband. I fear we may be an unmatched yoke, my lord."

"I, and your father, believe there is time to match our yoke and secure a kind of happiness. You would want for little. We would each have our own devices, keeping us busy and merry in turn."

"My father has agreed upon it with you?"

"He proposed it."

Beatrice paused, looking down at her father in the garden. "At his wish, I will wed."

The preparations for the masquerade had hardly been cleared away when preparations for the double wedding began. Hero's joy was matched only by Beatrice's somber acquiescence.

Beatrice's usual vigor and humor drained, day by day, and she retreated ever more often to quiet corners of the house with her diary or her books. Hero, knowing the heartbroken source of her cousin's reticence, quietly assumed more of the planning and preparations.

In a dull gray day dress, Beatrice sat on a dull red cushion and periodically looked out upon the dull green grass of the dull blue morning.

She composed verse as she lingered in the window seat of a dusty, disused salon. She wrote, as she usually had in recent days, of Sir Benedick. She was still unsure whether the specter at the ball was real, but she grew more certain with each passing day that it was him.

As she pondered a line whose rhythm was not quite right, muttering softly to herself and gazing through the window, the door opened and closed. Beatrice's gaze snapped up, but there was nobody there. Frowning, she laid her pencil in her diary, sitting up straighter. The room grew colder—dimmer.

"Benedick?" Beatrice said softly. She turned, swinging her legs down to face into the room. More certainly, she said, "Benedick. You never intimidated me in life, I'll hardly start fearing you in death."

Suddenly, there he was. Wearing his uniform. Tall, handsome, and cocksure as ever, he stood by the door. They stared silently at one another. As Beatrice looked, she noticed he was not quite solid; she could see through him, ever so slightly, to the heavy oak door.

Then he smiled. Achingly familiar, the smug smile sparked an equally familiar fire of mischief in her. She rose. "I always said you should quit your talking, for no one marks you. Now no one but me marks you at all. That must be worse for you than death."

"You are yet living, Lady Disdain." His smile did not fade.

Beatrice took a step toward him. "Disdain could never die with such food as you, Sir Benedick." She stopped several strides away from him, peering in disbelief. "And, whether a mad concoction of my own mind or not, I find you still in my disdainful presence."

"I would my horse had the speed of your tongue; perhaps I could then be truly in your presence."

Beatrice stepped, again, closer. "You speak like Benedick."

"I have never claimed to be another."

Beatrice laughed. "At the ball? You denied even knowing Benedick."

"It was a masquerade." Somehow, his eyes still twinkled with humor.

Beatrice finally closed the distance, pressing a hesitant hand to Benedick's cheek. A biting cold sunk to the bone and she recoiled quickly. She grew serious. "How can you be here, Benedick? You are dead."

He grew serious, too. "I felt I must see you again. I dared not to hope that you loved me; we quarreled ever while I lived. But I see your sadness; I have heard the counsel of Hero, Don Pedro, your uncle, and your father. It can be no trick. It seems your affections are true." He took a step toward her. She did not withdraw. "As I always said I would, I have died a bachelor; but here you are, my fair lady, and I cannot leave you behind. I do love you."

Beatrice could find not the breath to respond. The dreadful cold of the room and Benedick's overture combined to steal the air from her lungs. She gripped her diary tightly.

Then, from the corridor, Hero's voice: "Beatrice?"

"She comes to bid me to dinner," she told Benedick, still breathless.

"Then you must go."

"I would bid you join, but you have no stomach."

Benedick laughed; it lacked the luster it had once glittered with. "Fair Beatrice, I thank you for your pains."

"I took no more pains for those thanks than you take pains to thank me." So strange, to make fun as they always had; but strangely comforting.

From the hall again, and closer: "Beatrice? Where have you gone?"

"Farewell, my Beatrice." With a smile and before she could breathe another reply, Benedick vanished once more. The cold did not fade, so she was sure he still inhabited it; but the door opened and through it marched Hero, looking bewilderedly about.

"To whom did you speak, cousin?" Hero's own forehead was creased as she placed a hand against hers. "You are cold. Are you again unwell?"

Beatrice smiled. "I spoke only to myself. I was working out a verse. Shall we go down to dinner?"

Hero peered once more about the room. "Yes. Let us go."

Benedick did not always make himself visible to Beatrice, but she grew increasingly aware of his presence. A flicker in a mirror's corner, a shadow behind Don Pedro at dinner, a cold wind blowing through a corridor.

They had no time for conversation, much to her distress. She longed to speak to him again. There were, regrettably, wedding preparations to attend to and Don Pedro's attentions to humor. He was a good man, and though she was not eager to be forever manacled to him, she could not ignore him outright. Still, whenever possible, she removed herself from the business of the house to be alone.

It was such a time now, and she strolled in the garden. The morning was gray, but no rain fell, and the air was fresh and invigorating. She had not walked long, though, before she heard voices through a hedge.

"Are you certain Benedick was in love with her?" Ursula was asking.

"Yes," sighed Hero. "My own Claudio reports it, and Don Pedro says it is partly out of friendship that he feels the duty to see after her, with Benedick gone."

"Does she know?"

"No, and she never will," Hero said. "While Benedick lived, she was too proud and contemptuous to notice him; and now that he is dead, she wrestles with her mournful heart. It would only plunge her deeper into darkness to know that her love was requited."

"If she had known it in time, she would only have made endless sport of it," Margaret said wryly.

"You speak true," said Hero. "In any case: it is best that she never hear of it. I worry for her, but still hope she will emerge with close to the happiness she possessed before. We must do all we can to bestow her affections now on Don Pedro. Come, let us inside. I would like your opinion on some jewels."

Then the three were gone. A slow smile spread across Beatrice's face. "I grow ever surer my ghostly Benedick is real, and he speaks truly," she muttered. "Benedick, love on. I do requite you entirely."

After a while, Margaret returned, calling Beatrice's name. She did not reply but allowed Margaret to find her. Seeing the hedge by which she stood, alarm colored her face."How long have you stood here in the garden?"

"Only a few moments," Beatrice said, smiling faintly. "Why do you seek me?"

"Your wedding gown is nearly finished. You are needed for another fitting."

Beatrice's smile, and the levity of her heart, sunk at the reminder of her impending marriage. She had all but forgotten, Benedick's love so imposingly to mind. "Of course," she said. "Lead on."

The pair just beat the rain as they reached the glass doors from a parlor to the garden; fat drops began to fall heavily. Margaret pulled the doors against the swiftly gathering torrent. "How quickly the weather turns of late," she whinged. "I only wish for some sunshine."

Beatrice allowed herself to be led through dim halls and to the fitting room. When they arrived, the room was in an uproar. It was also uncomfortably cold despite a fire roaring in the hearth and all the windows and drapes firmly shut. Not paying any heed to the chatter, Beatrice looked about, knowing he was there. Only after she turned a full circle did she see him, walking down the hall, away from the room.

Darting to the door and clutching the jamb, she watched him go. "Benedick," she called. He stopped, turning to smile at her, then vanished.

Margaret's hand on her shoulder returned Beatrice to the present moment. Margaret quickly covered her consternation. "Your dress has been damaged. We aren't sure how it was so stained and torn while Hero's remains unscathed. The seamstress can run up a new one, still, in time for the wedding, but it will be quite the trick. I'm afraid it will be a longer fitting today, as she will have to drape almost an entirely new gown."

Beatrice's blood rushed in her ears, her heart thundering and hands trembling. Margaret's words seemed to slip through the air, difficult to apprehend, so there was a pregnant pause before she could formulate a proper reply. "That's alright. Would you fetch my book? I would like something to do."

"Of course."

Margaret disappeared down the hall and Beatrice was ushered onto a stool. The tattered remains of the dress were put over her head before the seamstress began to rip away unsalvageable sections.

Margaret returned and Beatrice gratefully accepted her book. She leafed through the pages to where she had last left off, then froze. Tucked within the pages was a note:

The god of love,
That sits above,
And knows me, and knows me,
How pitiful I deserve—

The verses were scribbled over, with lines tried over and again before the poor fragment of poetry was left abandoned. In the lower left corner, in the same hand, was written:

I cannot show love in rhyme. There, I have tried,
and you see the poor result. But well I love you;
I cannot bear to see you married to another.
Your Benedick

Beatrice stared at the writing. The seamstress, her assistant, and Margaret all looked at her unmoving, pale face with concern and tried to gain her attention. It took several repetitions of her name before she finally looked up.

"I-I suddenly suffer a fierce headache," she said. "Might I retire?"

The other women exchanged anxious glances. "We have your measurements and the old gown," the seamstress said finally. "Go rest yourself."

Beatrice sat alone in a front pew of the chapel. There had been a meeting to discuss the wedding; Hero and Claudio would recite their vows and be joined first. The wedding was in a mere two days. Beatrice had stayed behind; she was unsure how long it had just been her and the hollowness of the empty chapel. She, stared numbly at the altar where she would be tied forever to a man she felt nothing but mild respect for.

The candles guttered and the room grew suddenly cold. She knew without looking that Benedick sat beside her. She said nothing, continuing to gaze vacantly at the altar.

The icy touch of his fingers settled heavily on her wrist. She looked over at him then, blinking in surprise at a darkness in his eyes; they no longer looked as they had in life. They were almost entirely pupil, inky black. But his smile was the same, and she was happy to see him again. She did not pull back.

"Sweet Beatrice," he said, "would you come when I call you?"

"Yes. And stay until you bid me go," she said, meaning it.

"Stay with me until then," he said urgently, drawing near her face.

An amused smile flashed over Beatrice's lips, and she stood as if to leave. "Since 'then' has now been uttered, I had better be off."

Benedick's icy grip tightened on her wrist. "No. Stay."

Beatrice sat again. "It was only a jest."

"Tell me," he said, "for which of my foul parts do you love me?"

Beatrice hesitated, warring with her first inclination, which was to deny her love outright. She looked long at his face and beyond to the stained glass that shone faintly through it. She smiled and answered, "For all of them together do I suffer love for you."

"Suffer love; a good epithet," he said wryly. "I suffer in love, too. I suffer the more to see you marry another." A dark emotion flashed across Benedick's face and his hand grew colder on Beatrice's wrist.

"I suffer to do it," she confessed. "But I have little choice."

"Unite yourself with me."

Beatrice laughed, without thinking otherwise. There was, however, no mirth in Benedick's ghostly face. "I wish daily that I could. But you are dead, and I live. Death parts even those who married in life; the opportunity for our union has passed."

"It may be that we can't marry," he acknowledged. "But we may still be joined as one."

She withdrew her hand from his cold grip, brow furrowed. "Unless you can live again and find me here before two days pass," she said, "I must live the rest of my life with Don Pedro."

Anger flashed across Benedick's face. "I hate even to hear his name. And while I may have passed beyond living, you can still join me yet."

Beatrice stood and withdrew from the pew they shared, stopping before the altar. "You would rather see me dead than see me wed a friend?"

Benedick stood and crossed to her, taking her hands and gazing tenderly down at her. "I would rather you with me forever than in the arms of another. Don't you wish for the same?"

She stared. Then her heart softened. Finally, she murmured, "I do."

Gently, Benedick put his hands upon her cheeks. Beatrice did not shrink away from the cold or from his black eyes.

Her own eyes sank slowly closed and she whispered, "But I have made a promise."

"Yet you are mine." A frigid brush of his lips, like a cold morning mist, pressed against hers. Then his coldness vanished.

When Beatrice opened her eyes, she was alone, but a chill remained, deep in her breast. Votive candles flickered behind blue glass. A bell struck the hour: three o'clock. The sacred heart, dripping blood where the thorny crown pierced it, stared down at her. She stood for a long while, unable to move.

Perhaps that was the last she had seen of her Benedick; of her ghost. Her chilled heart ached at the thought.

※

A scream tore through the house. Beatrice sat straight up, having lain awake, tortured by thoughts of her wedding on the morrow. Her heart hammered; the throaty scream was a man's. Leaping from bed, she pulled on a dressing gown and snatched up a candle before flying down the corridors to where Don Pedro slept.

She quickly arrived and flew through his door. The room was cold, though growing warmer, and her candle guttered as a draft passed her and disappeared into the hall. She looked over her shoulder, into the dark, but saw no sign of her ghost. She rushed to a gasping Don Pedro. "My lord?" Beatrice set her candle down at his bedside.

Don Pedro struggled to sit, clutching at his throat. Beatrice saw the cold, white imprint of a hand, slowly fading, under where his own fingers splayed as he gasped for breath.

"I awoke to a heaviness on my chest, heavy as a man, and a burning coldness at my throat. I could not breathe. I fought against it and threw something off. It quickly overcame me again but has vanished since you entered. I cannot tell what it was; I am sure there was no one else in the room."

Others filed into the room. "A fit of some kind, perhaps?" Leonato said, sounding uncertain.

"I hear that wartime experiences can cause such terrors, especially after dark," Beatrice suggested weakly.

Don Pedro shook his head, looking pale and shaken.

"Let us see your throat," Claudio said, drawing near. Beatrice picked up her candle and stepped aside. When Don Pedro lifted his hand, the white handprint she had seen had vanished. The men exchanged a worried look, but agreed it was likely nothing more than a nightmare.

"We rise early tomorrow," Leonato said. "Let us all try to sleep. I will post a man by your door, Don Pedro." He turned to Beatrice. "To bed with you. Your bridegroom is well. You will see him again soon enough."

Beatrice, feeling little comforted, nodded shakily and retreated down the corridors. Back in her own room, she did not blow out the candle, sitting among her blankets, her knees drawn to her chest. To distract herself, she retrieved her diary.

You may marry him tomorrow; but I will love you evermore.
Yours, Benedick

A feeling of desperation welled in her and fell in a tear down her cheek. She drifted to sleep upright, diary clutched to her chest, and slept fitfully.

Hero buzzed joyfully all that morning as the brides readied in the chamber, though Beatrice was pale and quiet. Her gown was finished and undamaged. Hero had selected jewels for her neck and flowers for her hair. A veil shrouded her eyes and cascaded elegantly down her back.

Looking in the mirror, she thought with an amused twitch of her lips that she looked white as a ghost. Hero came to stand beside Beatrice. Beatrice smiled at her cousin's reflection, as swathed in white as she but rosy and vibrant with happy anticipation.

"You are the most beautiful of brides, fair cousin."

"As are you," Hero replied, nudging her with her shoulder. "I am happy that we share the day."

Beatrice smiled but said nothing.

It was in a daze that she allowed Margaret to lift her train and help her through the passages of the old house. Still numb, Beatrice was arranged outside the chapel doors alongside Hero. Together, they walked down the deceptively short aisle. The peerage of Messina looked on. Don Pedro and Beatrice nodded to one another, and Hero and Claudio began to recite their vows.

When it was done, Claudio and Hero shared a joyful kiss. Bells rang and the onlookers clapped and cheered. The sound slowly died away as Hero and Claudio turned beaming faces upon Beatrice and Don Pedro.

Beatrice's blood rushed in her ears as she faced her betrothed at the altar. He took her shaking hands gently and offered her a reassuring smile which she could not return. The priest's voice echoed faintly in her ears, as though far away. Beatrice looked out upon the congregation. Scores of eyes looked back, hope and concern intermingled in their gazes. She scanned those faces until her gaze was caught by eyes nearly black. Face gaunter than she recalled, and looking as solid as she had yet seen him, Benedick's ghost stood solemnly at the back of the chapel.

Don Pedro's voice rumbled in her unhearing ears. Her hands slipped, limp, from his grasp. Benedick looked at her, then to Don Pedro. A flash of rage contorted his features into something horrible, but vanished so swiftly that Beatrice was unsure of her sight.

Clear as the bells, his voice rang through the chapel: "My love, I have had thee."

Beatrice turned to him, looking out over the congregation, who now contemplated her in bafflement. She looked to Don Pedro and the priest, staring as they awaited her answer to the vows she had hardly heard the priest pose.

Desperately, she took Don Pedro's arm. "Do you not see him?" She pointed to where Benedick stood. He was no longer there. She looked again; now he stood at the end of the aisle between pews, mere strides away, gaze fixed steadily on her. Dropping her hand from Don Pedro, she stepped toward Benedick.

"Benedick, I love you," she said. "But you must let me do this. My heart breaks, but death took you and left me behind."

"I can't see you wed another," he said gravely.

Frantically, she looked out to the congregation. Leonato and Antonio were standing. Margaret and Ursula exchanged wide-eyed looks. Turning to the altar, Beatrice reached first toward Hero and then Don Pedro. "You must see him. You must hear him."

"Who, cousin?" Hero's voice shook.

"Benedick!" She turned to Don Pedro. "Your friend. Your soldier. He stands here, even now! He has haunted the halls of the house all this time, appearing to me, speaking to me. He destroyed the dress, he attacked you last night. He has been with me all the while and I cannot —I cannot—I cannot marry."

Antonio was at her side, taking her arm. Hero, Claudio, and Don Pedro all stepped back and the church was quiet with unease.

"Daughter," Antonio said softly. "You imagine."

"Was it imagination that strangled you last night?" Beatrice said to Don Pedro. "Benedick is here. He is my love, and a jealous one. I respect you, Don Pedro. I appreciate the honor of this match. But I am the wife of Benedick; I cannot match with another. He cannot stand to see me match with another. We would be unhappy and you would be unsafe. He is only content with me at his side; when we are parted, he is dangerous."

"Hush, now," Antonio whispered urgently, holding her a little tighter. To the crowd, he said, with a forced smile, "I am afraid we will have to end the day with only one happy union. I hope to welcome you back for Beatrice's joyous nuptials on a sunnier day." With that, he escorted her back down the aisle.

Benedick glided close by her side.

"How I love you," he said softly. "We shall be together."

Beatrice clung to her father's arm, her knees weak as he half-carried her from the chapel. "Why can they not see you? Why do you show yourself only to me? They think me mad. Show yourself, Benedick. Tell them. Tell them you will not have me marry another."

"None but you can see me, my love. Only your eyes can see the truth."

Overwhelmed and trembling, darkness submerged Beatrice and she knew nothing more.

She awoke alone. She recognized the room as her hastily prepared chamber in her father's countryside manor. She must have slept long to have been transported all the way there. Most of the furniture was still shrouded in large, white sheets. The air was still, stale, and dusty. Turning her head, she saw a letter at the bedside.

Bea,

You took quite ill. Don Pedro and I have agreed that it was no match, after all. You are not ready to wed; not so soon after the news of Benedick, who does appear to haunt your memory. I have brought you to the country to rest peacefully. I will return in a few hours' time; I must arrange for staff and goods. Rest. I will see you soon.

Father

Slowly, Beatrice got out of bed. She pulled on a dressing gown and walked down to the kitchen. Rummaging through cupboards, she found an old tin of tea, some hardened sugar, and bundles of kindling for the stove. Ah, and some arsenic; the country house always struggled with rats. The kettle sat on the stove. Filling it, she stoked the fire that had already been started, presumably by her father.

Behind her, a sudden draft of cold gusted. She didn't even turn. "Hello, Benedick." The coldness was upon her, freezing arms wrapped about her waist and icy lips pressed a kiss to her neck.

"My Beatrice."

"You are who I wish to be with. You are the husband I was meant to have." She turned. He was her Benedick, ever handsome, ever witty. He would be by her side forever. Not even death could part them.

"Will you come to be with me? Forever my own?" he asked, almost disbelieving. He smiled and fetched her hand to kiss it. His grasp seemed to leech some of her own warmth, but she was unbothered, smiling at the affectionate touch.

"There is naught left for me here," she replied. "All Messina thinks me mad. And I am, in a way, I suppose. Mad for love; mad for loss. Mad for longing. In his letter, Father pretends that I may one day emerge normal. It cannot be. No husband would have me and no one will ever be able look on me as they once did." She looked up at him with a small smile. "Even if another husband could be found, I don't believe you would let him stay long."

"No, I would not," Benedick snarled, his features contorting as anger flashed through cold eyes.

There was that look again; it should frighten her, she knew. Before it could, it was gone, and in its place was only her lovely Benedick.

The kettle whistled. Beatrice turned, scooping the arsenic and some sugar into her cup before she poured the boiling water into the teapot, stirring it well. Benedick watched in solemn silence.

"No milk. A shame, but one must make do," Beatrice said playfully. She took the tea to the table and sat, watching the swirling steam rise. She continued to look, frozen, until the steam disappeared, and the tea grew cool.

Benedick looked on. "Why do you wait? We are so close to forever."

"I find myself afraid to die. It is ever so final." She looked to Benedick, to fortify herself, and lifted the cup toward her lips. Benedick looked on in eager anticipation. At the last moment, she lowered it. She turned to look at him again, apologetic. "Benedick—"

A sharp pain.

She dropped the cup. Looking down, she saw the handle of a kitchen knife buried in her center. Crimson blood bloomed, like spreading petals across her pale dressing gown. She looked up into Benedick's spectral face, now changed. All rotting sinew and bone, his lips stretched oddly around a sinister smile, his eyes all black. Frantic fear froze her heart even as it slowed, weakly pulsing.

"I will have you. Out of pity, I force your hand."

Beatrice gaped at him in horror. Her head lolled on a weak neck. She grew paler by the moment. Her lips blued and her gaze blurred.

Benedick's skeletal fingers reached for her. His arms wrapped around her and lifted her, holding her limp form close. Beatrice dimly realized that he no longer felt cold.

"Let's have a dance before we are joined."

As the lifeblood drained slowly from Beatrice's failing heart, Benedick turned them in lazy circles about the kitchen. The deadly tea lay, spilled and forgotten, upon the table.

WE, UNHAPPY
(THE TWO GENTLEMEN OF VERONA)
SABRINA HOWARD

Launce sliced his knife through the flesh of the strawberry in his hand and watched the juice trickle down his fingers like blood. When he looked up, his dog was watching him, sad eyes fastened on the fruit.

"I have oft said you were the sourest dog e'er there was. Yet methinks you are the happiest among us now." Launce sighed, tossing the strawberry into Crab's waiting mouth.

The only pleasure Launce found in Milan was to be away from his master, Proteus. Even so, those moments could hardly be called pleasure. They were relief—from Proteus's presence, from cold commands, from an atmosphere so devoid of love as to be sharp and glass-like with indifference. In his master's house, Launce was burdened with distaste on his tongue and pity on his shoulders for the lady Julia, who could no more find faithfulness in Proteus than sin in God.

Launce plucked another strawberry from the basket in his lap, sliced off the leaves, and ate it. He let himself linger in its sweetness, the warmth of the afternoon sun, the birdsong that suffused the air around him.

He closed his eyes and imagined himself in Verona, where the sun-struck waters lapped against the stone walk, the streets were familiar, and the people intimate. He would walk the garden with his sister, give scratches to the cat, and wish his mother and father goodnight when dusk melted to darkness.

The crunch of boots on the dirt path disrupted Launce's daydream. Milan again.

Proteus.

"How now! Asleep while there is work to be done?"

"Not asleep, sir," said Launce, turning to Proteus, "yet dreaming still." The taste in his mouth turned sour and he tossed the last of the strawberries to Crab.

Proteus regarded the mutt with an unfeeling stare before leveling the same gaze on Launce. "Hie thee to Valentine and deliver this message," he said, producing a letter. When Launce reached for it, Proteus jerked it back. "With clean hands."

Launce looked down at his fingers, stained blood red. He set his knife aside, wiped his hands clean, and took the letter, mollified to be sent to the honorable Valentine. "I will go at once."

Proteus nodded and turned away without another word.

Launce retrieved his knife and watched his master go, idly imagining following Proteus and plunging the knife into his back. Launce could return to Verona. Julia could find a more worthy husband. Neither Milan nor Verona would be worse for his absence.

Crab padded forward and laid his dirty snout in Launce's lap.

"'Tis merely a thought," Launce said, stowing the knife in his boot. "Not a whit more."

Milan's marketplace thrummed with life and energy, and Silvia threaded between the stalls with a smile. Her handmaid followed, armed with a woven basket bearing bolts of fine silk, lemons and oranges, lilies and sunflowers.

A stand of leather craftsmanship caught Silvia's eye and she approached, thinking of a gift for Valentine. The heady aromas of leather and oil surmounted the other scents of the market—the drifting smoke of cooked meats, the lighter notes of fruits and florals, the earthy mix of woodwork, sweat, and spices. She leaned forward to examine a small leather pouch, its exterior finely tooled with a pattern of violets and carnations. Faithfulness and love, utterly befitting her dear husband.

As she made the purchase and set the pouch in the basket, her handmaid cleared her throat. "Perhaps," she said, "my lady would prefer to venture to another part of the market?"

"Wherefore?" Silvia asked.

Her maid's eyes flicked to a spot in the distance.

Silvia turned.

The lady Margaret, visiting from Venice, stood illuminated in a patch of sunlight that cut through the canopy of colorful fabric hung above the vendors' stalls. She was arrayed in a fine dress of purple hues, her attention fixed on a gentleman angled away from Silvia.

For a moment, Silvia was confused; she had taken no issue with Margaret, and indeed had enjoyed making her acquaintance since her arrival three days past. Then the gentleman shifted and the afternoon sun cast his face in bronze.

Proteus.

Silvia's stomach churned and she fought the urge to flee, planting her heels on the cobbled path. He lifted a hand to touch Margaret's elbow, his features aglow with passion.

She shuddered in memory of that same look, the same unrelenting want in his dark heart. She recalled the ease with which he'd proclaimed both his betrothed Julia and his friend Valentine to be dead—when both were alive and well—in a shameless attempt to defraud his way into her heart. Heat flushed through her, muscles tightening at the ghost of his hands upon her in the forest outside Mantua.

Love 'gainst the nature of love, he said.

His fingertips, pressed into the skin of her forearms.

The stink of his breath.

The madness that moved in the depths of his eyes, like worms pushing up from rotten earth.

Silvia's jaw was clenched so tightly that her teeth ached. Valentine may have forgiven Proteus, but she could not—could never. Now here he was, repeating his offenses, lavishing his attentions on yet another woman.

"My lady?" Silvia's maid's voice was tinny and faint above the roaring of blood in her ears.

She turned her back on Proteus. "Find Julia. Ask her to accompany me in the Duke's gardens presently."

Her maid curtsied and departed, and Silvia spared one last look at Proteus.

He was laughing.

She abhorred that laugh.

❦

Julia strolled beside Silvia in the Duke's gardens, their steps measured and slow over a soft pathway of Roman chamomile. Rose bushes hemmed them in from either side, the leaves and thorns and silken petals dampening the words that passed between them. They two could know the substance of their conversation, and no one else.

Speaking freely and in earnest, Silvia relayed what she had seen in the marketplace and Julia received it without surprise. She had known Proteus's mind from his first meeting with the lady Margaret. He desired her, as he had once desired Julia—and Silvia too.

Between Proteus and the object of his desire, there was no obstacle too great to surmount. Julia had been an obstacle herself, as his betrothed, when he'd fallen for Silvia. Now, as his wife, she was an obstacle again.

Julia rubbed at the ring he'd given her, a gold band embossed with an intricate floral pattern and the words *AMOR VERUS* inscribed on the inside. *Love true.*

Proteus understood only half that sentiment.

The garden path turned, leading the two women to an intersection with a large sundial in its center. They paused before it, and Julia fancied she could see the shadows moving, time stalking forward like a fiend from the darkness.

"Do you think," Silvia asked, her tone low, "that Proteus will stray so far off the path of decency in pursuit of the lady Margaret as he did for me?"

"I do," Julia said. In fact, she suspected he would go farther. The weight of those suspicions hung from her shoulders, coiled around her chest like some slow instrument of death.

Silvia shook her head. "How quickly you and Valentine were dead to Proteus, once he wanted me." The set of her face was hard, but her features softened as she turned to Julia. "I wonder…" She hesitated, glancing back at the sundial.

"Speak," Julia said, offering a wry smile. "You can say nothing slanderous about my husband which I have not thought myself."

Silvia's lips quirked, then the humor drained from her expression. She laid a hand on Julia's arm. "I wonder how far the distance is from wishing your friends dead, to making them so."

Cold fear traced the curve of Julia's spine, running down her back like a lover's touch. If Silvia was of a similar mind, perhaps her own suspicions were truly sound. Perhaps her fears had come not from imagination, but from insight.

"Proteus has made plans," Julia whispered, "to journey to Mantua—the two of us, alone."

Silvia's breath caught. "Then if he does wish you dead—"

"It will be the perfect time to kill me." Julia nodded. She had indeed read him true.

The very evening Proteus had first met Margaret, Julia had found him on his way out of the stables, on the point of hanging a heavy rope on a hook. They had made eye contact, then his gaze had dropped to the braided rope in his hands.

They were the only two in the stables and the courtyard outside had been empty, filling second by second with darkness. The stench of manure and hay stuffed Julia's lungs like cotton.

When Proteus looked up again, his eyes were cold, and she knew they were wondering the same thing. Would he kill her, right now, like this?

He entertained the thought for a moment longer before his lips pulled into a mirthless smile and he replaced the rope on the hook. He swept past her, close enough to stir the hair around her face. She had stayed there, trembling, until night had drawn its cloak around Milan.

"I am glad," Julia said, taking Silvia's hands in hers, "that you see what I see in him. I have been pondering what action to take. I would hear your advice."

Silvia drew closer. "My dear Valentine must never hear word of this, for Proteus is still his childhood friend and holds a place in his heart. But—for your own safety, for the wrongs he has done, and for the rotten deeds he may yet accomplish—I believe we must needs pay him back in kind." She met Julia's gaze and held it fast. "If he intends to kill you, you must kill him first."

At dinner, Julia sat across from Proteus and pondered the ways he might kill her. She let the conversation in the Duke's hall wash over her, engaging where necessary, but fixing her attention on her husband. He smiled at Margaret the way he had once smiled at her—and at Silvia. Hopeful. Charming. Love-drunk.

It had not been long after their wedding when, on viewing her, he lost that look. His eyes emptied, his heart shriveled, and his mind searched elsewhere. This time, he had found his elsewhere in Margaret.

It all played out in Julia's mind—the events that would occur following her death on the route to Mantua, should Proteus's schemes succeed. He would make a show of mourning for his wife. Then he would take Margaret for his own; if she were not won over by his charms as Julia had been, she would be forced, as Silvia had nearly been. And, once they were wed, his affections would wear thin. A new unfortunate woman would take the fearsome place in his dark heart, and Margaret would be the next to fall.

"Sweet Julia." Valentine's warm address pulled her from her musings; she curved her lips into a smile and turned to him. "I was delighted to hear of your travel plans. Mantua will be romantic indeed." He glanced at Proteus. "I am told the two of you intend to start your journey without any company, so that you may better rejoice in each other's presence."

"That is the truth of it, sir; we are to undertake a portion of the traveling alone." That was when Proteus would kill her; she was certain. Without witnesses, her death could be pinned on bandits. Wildlife. A mere tragic accident. Julia picked up her wine glass to obscure the tremor in her hands and cast a meaningful look at Silvia. "It will be a time rife with opportunity."

"Indeed." Valentine addressed Proteus with another question, but Julia did not listen. Their trip was an opportune time for her as well; if it was adequate cover for her own death, it would likewise be adequate for Proteus's, too.

Julia took to her roasted meat with renewed vigor, heart pounding. As she sliced, the candlelight glinted off the blade of her knife, yellow-white and hypnotizing. She paused and watched the inverted world in the silver, rotating her wrist to see the light dance. Her hands were steady now.

She looked up.

Proteus watched her. A tingling sensation blossomed in her chest, not unlike what she had felt when she'd read his love letter in Verona. *Love-wounded Proteus.*

Julia held his gaze and they smiled at each other—a challenge. Once again, their thoughts were the same. Would she kill him, right now, like this?

She imagined lunging across the table, spilling the wine and the gravy and the bowl of peas, and splitting his throat with her knife. His eyes, wide and horror struck. The artful spray of his blood over the Duke's fine linen.

Then she breathed out slowly and set the knife on her plate.

Patience.

Proteus's smile grew, and he turned to Valentine in answer to a remark Julia hadn't heard. "Ay," he said, "my lady has always had a commendable spirit."

Launce spattered through the summer eve's rain, marching like a soldier to war, and burst through the doors of his favorite local alehouse. Like never before in his life, his heart was cleaved—shredded with twin knives of grief and bloodlust.

Breathing heavily, he shouldered his way through the cheerful crowd, past the fiddlers on the tavern stage, and between wenches with sticky trays of beer steins running over with foam. In the far corner, at a table beneath a tapestry of the Duke's family crest, Valentine's servant Speed was waiting.

Speed half-stood and beckoned with a smile. "Launce! Good even!"

"Nay." Launce dropped into a seat across from him and covered his face with shaking hands. "A blacker evening I have never met."

"How now! What has happened?"

Launce ducked over the table, one sleeve growing damp with spilled ale. "You must ne'er repeat this news, upon your honor."

Speed leaned forward, nodding solemnly. "Upon my honor."

"I have this evening discovered a secret which my master Proteus has kept from me." He wrung his hands, pulling at the cuffs of his sleeves. "I have learned, from his correspondence with family in Verona, that my sister Ann"—he choked on her name and swallowed convulsively before plunging on—"has fallen deathly ill."

"O horror!" Speed covered his mouth with a hand. Through his fingers, he asked, "You are to Verona, then?"

"Marry, I am not! I cannot. My master would upbraid me should he find out I have spied on his letters. For certain he would not allow me to leave, otherwise he would not have kept this wounding secret." Launce cracked his knuckles, imagining breaking his hand on Proteus's face.

The noise of the alehouse raged on, yet Speed remained silent for many moments. "My friend," he said at last, "I have no words for thee. I am sorry. I shall pray for her soul."

Quiet thunks on the table made Launce look up. Mugs of ale and two small cakes sat between him and Speed.

"I have no appetite for cake," Launce said. His appetite now was for blood. Proteus had kept this secret from him and would never allow him to return home. Verona had grown cold in his master's eyes, and Launce feared he might never see his family again. Or indeed, sweet Ann.

"Drink, then," Speed suggested, nudging a mug forward.

Launce took it, knuckles white. "Thirst, at least, I have."

When he had drunk his fill and had wiled away some hours with his friend, Launce left the alehouse with a powerful certainty and a single purpose in his mind. He staggered through the darkened streets, splashing through mirrored pools of rainwater, the chill night air numbing the tips of his fingers. He did not stop until he reached the door to Proteus's rooms.

There was a light burning inside; the orange glow shimmered around the edges of the door, blurring the outline of the frame.

Launce doubled over and pulled the knife from his boot.

He reached for the bronze handle.

The door jerked open and the lady Julia was there. She drew back with a gasp, then gave a small laugh, the high notes strung with nervousness.

"Launce," she said, hand on her chest. "You startled me." Her eyes alighted on the knife, but she made no comment as he stowed it belatedly in his pocket.

"I am sorry, madam," he said. He blinked and tried to see the room over her shoulders, but she moved forward and shut the door behind her.

"Will you go with me to the kitchen? I have a mind to brew some tea and would appreciate the company. In these late hours, the shadows seem always to harbor some ill intention."

"Of course, my lady." Launce turned and followed her away from Proteus, focusing on walking as straight as possible. He could not very well rid himself of her husband now, not under her observation. He would accompany her and bide his time.

In the kitchen hearth, a fire blazed, warm and inviting. Launce drew up beside the flames and watched Julia move about, preparing tea. She could have asked Launce to do it, to bring it to her rooms. Perhaps she sought a moment away from Proteus, as Launce often did.

Or perhaps she smelled the ale on his breath and did not trust him to fetch tea.

In any case, she did not seem bothered by the task. Humming softly, she approached the bunches of dried flowers she'd strung upon the wall—roses, lavender, and other handsome varieties Launce couldn't name. She gathered several dried buds into a little cup, used a pestle to crush the petals, and took them to the countertop with care.

"The kettle, sir, if you would," she said, gesturing to the fire.

Launce grabbed a heavy cloth and removed the kettle from the fireplace, the bubbling of the water momentarily perceptible above the snapping of the flames.

Julia mixed the flower petals with tea leaves and measured precise scoops into a ceramic teapot. Then she stepped back and indicated the pot.

Launce poured hot water over the mixture and set the kettle on a block of wood on the countertop. Notes of lavender infused the air, and he thought again of Verona—the flowers in his mother's garden box, his sister selecting blooms and arranging them in a vase on the table.

Steam curled from the spout of the teapot.

Julia watched it too, leaning over the counter as she waited for the tea to steep, her chin cupped in one hand.

Launce sniffed. "Do you miss Verona, my lady?"

She looked at him and smiled, but there was something false about the curve of her lips. "There is much to love in Milan."

"I miss Verona." He pressed on, emboldened—or perhaps merely dulled—by drink. Julia, like him, had left Verona to follow Proteus.

Launce, for his part, was as loyal a servant as he must be—or rather, disloyal up to the point of punishment. He had packed up and left his family and his life in Verona to serve Proteus in Milan; he could not have done otherwise without severe consequences.

Julia, however, had followed him for love. She had disguised herself as a page boy, undertaken the journey to Milan, even gotten herself employed by Proteus without being discovered—all to chase after him, to hold onto his wandering love.

And how was that faring? Launce had seen the way his master was fastening himself to the lady Margaret, digging in by his teeth like a boil-brained leech.

"Do you regret it, madam?" The words slipped past his lips before he thought to stop them. Then, committed, he asked again: "Do you regret following your gentleman?"

He was wildly out of his place, and he waited for the scolding to start or for her hand to strike his face.

Neither came.

Instead she said, with the same care she used to harvest dead flowers, "It was not long ago that I made that decision, and yet methinks I was much younger then. Perhaps we all, in our youth, sow regrets for our older selves."

Launce furrowed his brows. He was on the edge of something, on the point of peeling back some mystery. Civility dictated that he hold his tongue, but curiosity dragged him onward. She had stepped around his question to avoid the answer. Perhaps, as his servant, she expected him to relay his information to Proteus.

Yet she had seen his knife. He was sure of it.

"I want to help," he said.

"With the tea?" Julia asked, busying herself with gathering cups, saucers, a silver strainer, cubes of sugar. "You have done so. However, when it is ready, you may save me the effort and take it in to Proteus."

"Not with the tea," Launce said. He swallowed. He could be killed for this. "With Proteus."

Julia's facade cracked and she turned to look at him, gray eyes alight. In the glow of the fire, or in the gleam of her veiled excitement, her beauty was heightened, the roses in her cheeks all a-bloom. Her hair was the same yellow hue as his sister's.

"Speak straight, Launce," she said, "so that I do not mistake your meaning. Nor you mine."

"I will be plain. If you intend to murder Proteus," he said, holding her gaze as he stooped to a bow, "then I wish to be of service."

She smiled, not in happiness, but with pleasure all the same. "Very well," she said. "Deliver the tea and tell Proteus that I am feeling unwell and must take some air. Then return here, and I will tell you the whole of our plans, as they stand so far."

"Ay, madam." He took up the tea tray with shaking hands. He may yet see his sister again. They would all be free of Proteus forever. "It is my honest pleasure to serve."

<hr />

Silvia took Valentine's hand and together they swept to the center of the Duke's hall to join the other dancers. Gentlemen and ladies milled about in pairs, finding a place and waiting for the music to begin. Margaret was here with a visiting gentleman from Genoa. Proteus and Julia were absent, preparing for their departure on the morrow.

A soft hand cradled her jaw—Valentine, turning her to face him. "You seem worried, my love. What ails you?"

"I confess I am thinking of Julia and Proteus. I bear some reservations about their journey to Mantua."

Valentine smiled. "I am pleased you have found such companionship in the lady Julia, even though you have not much history together, as Proteus and I have. It is sweet of you to think of her. But I assure you, you need not fret."

"Yet you have had adventures in that forest yourself and know of its dangers." They moved into their starting position, side by side, hands clasped. Silvia squeezed his fingers. "Tell me of them, that I may be informed."

The music began, and they moved to the slow moan of the violin, following the steps of the pavane.

"Will that knowledge not put you ill at ease?" Valentine asked.

"No," she said, "for I am given to imagine more and worse horrors than those that exist." She watched him as they revolved around each other, slow and steady. In truth, the forest's dangers might help them anticipate Proteus's plans. Though she, Julia, and Launce had their own strategy, they remained perilously unaware of Proteus's potential moves.

"Very well," Valentine said, when they had returned to each other's side. "I can tell you that the chances of encountering bandits are slim. Perhaps there may be savage wildlife, but Proteus will be armed with his rapier and will be well able to fend off an attack."

Silvia froze, then took the next step of the dance a half-second late. *His rapier.* Proteus could run her through with it.

Valentine continued; less familiar with the court dances that Silvia had grown up with, he had not noticed her misstep. "There are also various waterfalls and cliffs that may be hazardous, but you needn't concern yourself with those, either. I have marked them on a map for Proteus."

The two of them moved into another revolution and Silvia fought to conceal her fear as they circled face-to-face. "A map?" she asked, breathless. "For Proteus?" It was, verily, a handbook of convenient spots for murder.

"Ay." Valentine threaded his fingers through hers in a gesture of reassurance that had no effect. "Proteus wrote to me, to ask for my detailed assessment of the forest, so that he may avoid and prepare for danger. He came to retrieve the map personally and discussed it all with me. I can even tell you that he seemed nervous, or off in some way—and that is a good sign. It means he is taking the dangers of the forest and the safety of his love most seriously. I assure you, dear Silvia. Proteus is ready for whatever may come."

Silvia swallowed. She wondered if her husband could feel the cold sweat collecting on her palms. "That map," she said. "Have you another copy? I would be interested to look over it myself."

He laughed softly. "What need have you of maps, my dear? I promise: all will be well. Proteus and Julia will reach Mantua safely."

The dance drew to a close, and the music kicked into a livelier tempo—the galliard next.

Silvia forced herself to follow the steps, to smile and laugh with the others. Tonight was for merriment.

Tomorrow, murder.

The first rays of sunlight burnished the room in gold; Julia would have admired it under other circumstances. Today, however, it was a marker of time pressing forward, Fate leading her and Proteus into the forest, only one to return.

Apprehension bloomed in her chest, burrowed in her stomach like the gnarled roots of an ancient tree. She rolled her teacup in her hand, watching the dark liquid swirl within, but did not drink. She set it on the table, wiped her palms on her dress, and turned her gaze to Proteus.

He drank his tea and replaced it on the table, saying nothing.

Launce entered the room and set Proteus's bags at his feet. "Your things, sir," he said, stepping away and rocking on his heels. His eyes darted to Julia and back again. "I wish you safe passage. I will join you in Mantua in a day's time. Unless you wish me to join you sooner—"

"Silence, sirrah!" Proteus kneaded his forehead with his knuckles and glared at his servant. Then he took a deep breath and sat back in his chair with a show of comfort. "All will be well. You may leave us now."

Julia's hands tightened around fistfuls of her dress beneath the table, but she kept her features clear. She met eyes with Launce as he left. She wished she could have nodded to him, offering courage, but Proteus was studying her with unusual intensity.

At last, she could not bear his gaze, and leapt to her feet. "Shall we be off?"

Proteus stood slowly and gathered their bags with deliberation.

She wondered what he was planning, how he intended to kill her. His map gave him many options, too many for them to anticipate. Her eyes traced the sheath of his rapier, and she imagined what it would feel like—cold steel passing through her body.

Proteus strode to the door and held it open. "Come," he said. "Let us away."

Julia grabbed the bouquet of rhododendron flowers from the vase on the table. "For luck," she told Proteus, and she swept out the door ahead of him.

***

"We will pass by our spot in the forest, will we not?" Julia asked.

Proteus was silent for several seconds, and Julia followed him carefully, maintaining her distance. "Our spot?" he asked at last.

"Do you not recall? I refer to the clearing where we had our misadventures with Valentine and Silvia and the outlaws. I say it is our spot because it is where you remembered your love for me."

Bear witness, Heaven, he had said. *I have my wish for ever.*

And I have mine, Julia had said.

How quickly both their wishes had changed.

"Ay," he said. "We will pass the spot, and I will point it out to you."

When they reached the clearing, it all came back in razored detail. The scratchiness of her page costume. The weight of the two rings in her pocket—one Proteus had given to her in Verona, and one he had intended to give to Silvia. And Silvia, the disgust in her tone.

In love, who respects friends? Proteus had asked.

All men but Proteus.

Proteus slowed to a stop, caught his breath against the trunk of an alder tree. "It is here," he said, gesturing. "Our spot."

"Is it?" Julia asked, flippant. "Now that we are here, I can discern it not from any other part of these woods." She twisted the bunch of rhododendrons in her hand, scattering a few leaves to the ground, then fiddled with Proteus's ring instead. It was loose on her sweaty finger. She eyed his rapier and looked away again. "Perhaps we had best press on."

Proteus's gaze turned back the way they had come, to the empty forest left in their wake. There were no witnesses now, but this clearing was too close to civilization for murderous secrets; Julia had arrived at the same conclusion herself.

"Ay," he said. "We journey on."

Julia tore more petals from her flowers, waited for him to gain a head start, and followed.

They walked for longer than Julia expected, their pace growing slower and more meandering as they went. With each step, Julia's heart beat harder. She plucked petals one by one, waiting for Proteus to make a move.

It did not come. Not yet.

They stumbled over root-gnarled earth, and Julia realized that they were following the distant sound of water. It grew into a cheerful burble, and a stream came into view. It flowed down the mountainous forest to their right, spilling off the edge into a secluded waterfall.

Proteus dropped their bags beside a nearby boulder, panting slightly, and sat. Julia, keeping him in her sights, crossed the stream and strolled to the edge of the waterfall to look down. The drop was steep, the flow of water turning to mist before it hit the rocky bottom.

She backed away and gave her full attention to Proteus. "Why have we stopped?" she asked, shaking the last few petals out of her bouquet and tossing the stems into the stream.

Proteus gave a strained laugh. "I think you know," he said. "You made a fool of me once, with your page disguise, but I have known your cleverness since then. Do not think I will miss a trick again."

Julia smiled. It was a relief to have it all out in the open. "And what of *your* tricks?"

"Indeed, I have them," he said, leaning back on the boulder. "And I confess to one now: I intend to be rid of you, my love. Presently."

"Then I must confess to you as well," she said. "I have known your intentions for some time, dear Proteus. Surely you cannot have mistaken mine."

He sat up, grinning. "We are in contest, then."

"You mistake me, husband." Her heartbeat crescendoed in her ears, a heady thrill coursing through her veins. She strode forward, until her feet splashed into the gentle stream between them. "I have won already."

"Won!" He scoffed. "Where is your victory, when I stand here still?" His fingers curved around the hilt of his rapier. "Perhaps, dear Julia, you are simply not bold enough for blood."

"Perhaps *you* are not calm enough for cleverness. Tell me, have you not been feeling poorly these last few days?"

He laughed again, but the sound was splintered, fractured on the sharp edges of his nerves. "You mean to claim a paltry illness as your handiwork?"

"Indeed, although it is not paltry—not for long. I expect you are feeling somewhat more poorly today."

Proteus shot to his feet, then stumbled before regaining his footing. "You devil! What have you done?"

The taste of triumph was as pleasurable as the finest wine in Milan. She drew closer to him as he began to sway on his feet. "Proteus, did you see me drink my tea this morning?"

The little color left in his face washed away. "You poisoned it."

"Ay," she said, "with dried foxgloves. A beautiful flower, yet lethal."

Proteus shook, fists clenched at his sides. "My sweet Julia," he spat, "if you would be my end, then I would be yours." He staggered toward her, sloshing into the stream too. He unsheathed his rapier, the hiss of metal ringing in the chill air.

Julia recoiled.

"Did you think you could win against me, woman?" he asked. "You, all alone?" He advanced on her, but she held her ground, lifted her head high.

"No," she said. "Not alone."

Proteus drew his rapier back, but before he could lunge, his body jerked. He cried out and fell, dropping to his knees in the stream, the rapier clattering onto slick wet stones.

Launce stood behind him, his knife stuck in Proteus's back.

Silvia removed the rapier from Proteus's reach.

"Are you alright, my lady?" Launce asked.

"I am well." Julia leaned down and plucked the knife from Proteus's back, earning a weak groan from him. His blood spooled into the water, threads of vermillion drawn away toward the falls. She handed the weapon back to Launce.

They watched Proteus struggle to get away from them, edging closer to the waterfall.

"Now," Silvia said, "we make an end of it." She splashed into the water and grabbed one of Proteus's arms, hauling him to the cliff. Julia and Launce joined her, pulling and pushing him until he lay, wheezing, mere inches from the drop.

Julia placed a shoe against Proteus's back, and Launce and Silvia followed suit.

"Goodbye, Proteus," said Julia and, as one, they shoved him over the edge.

Silvia doubled over, resting her hands on her knees, a grim half-smile on her features. "It is done," she said. "No one will have to fear his treachery again." She straightened and pulled Julia into a hug. "You and Launce may return to Verona soon. I pray you will be happy there."

Julia rubbed at her ring and regarded the spot where Proteus had vanished. Cold mist swirled in the backdraft, creating an eerie haze.

"O, unhappy, I am sure," she said. "And yet, victorious."

TO MAKE THE DEVIL'S BLOOD RUN COLD

(ROMEO AND JULIET)

MATHEW L REYES

The sins of Capulet and Montague I had borne well, as must we all bear the whims of the powerful; yet when they trod upon my father and sent him to an early grave, I vowed a vengeance that might make the Devil's blood run cold.

Though, why do I write *they*, when it is not some other entity to whom this narrative is addressed? No, it is to *you*, so-called 'Lord' Capulet and to *you*, so-called 'Lord' Montague, that I write these words. Read them, take them into your hearts, and know it was I who reduced to rubble your pillars of joy. It was not cruel fate, but I who salted the earth with your family's blood and withered the vine so no more flowers may bloom from it.

But I am ahead of myself.

Let me savor each word, each letter, as memory carries me through the sweetness of it all. Let every tear your families shed, every bestial wailing upon the caskets of their children, sustain me, fill my breast with joy.

I shall start at the beginning.

Fair Verona they call it, but if fair it be then fouler I would prefer. For there is an honesty in foulness that cannot be hidden, and in fairness a mask which hides gruesome deeds. And if fairness truly exists, then fair it is *only* for those at the top of Verona's ruling class. Prince Escalus, that vermin, who allows those of Houses Capulet, Montague, Scaligeri, Ordelaffi, and so many others to get away with crimes that would send an ordinary man to the stocks or gallows, is the top of the rot. Yes, Verona is fair—for their ilk only.

A street brawl killed my father. I need not bother you with the details other than that Capulet and Montague were at the center of it and that it occurred when I was a boy, only a bit older than Romeo Montague was when he first crossed my path.

I petitioned the Prince, Escalus's father, to do *something*, to render some justice for my family. It was a hot day when I begged him, on the steps of the Basilica di San Zeno Maggiore, to accept my petition.

"My father made my family's income," I pleaded, "and the brawl between those two beastly youths of Capulet and Montague, it frightened my father's horse, threw him from the saddle, and upon the yellow stones he broke his neck."

The Prince, his face aglow with colored light from the Basilica's rose window, as though he were ordained by God himself to rule Verona, gave me a piteous look but deigned not to speak to me.

He left me upon the steps.

It was there that I cursed the Lord our God, and it was there that I spotted the abbey which abutted the cathedral. I wanted nothing to do with that which had forsaken me, with a God that had allowed my family to be all but destroyed by the power of Verona. I was but a boy, barely able to grow the scruff of a beard; yet now I had to be a man and support my mother and two sisters without any recompense or help from the Prince.

I determined that I would face the hardships God had sent to me.

Can you imagine, Lords Capulet and Montague, what it is to struggle for years to put bread upon the table, to work yourself to the bone and have nothing to show for it but reduced circumstances? Had I not cursed God on that day, would things have been different? I don't know.

But the merchants my father had traded with abandoned us, would not take me on. We were swindled of our last coin, and by the end of the year following my father's murder—yes! I call it *murder* by the animals Capulet and Montague!—we were forced to live in the foulest part of Verona. Where once we had green gardens in the summer and a little harvest in the autumn, we now had dirty alleys smelling of excrement, a scent which permeated our clothing. I still smell it today.

Had we kept our home, would we have escaped the plague that swept through the destitute? Would my mother and sisters have succumbed to the black and bloody pustules, heaped upon death carts and dumped without ceremony into pits beyond Verona? One can never know.

But when the Death swept through the city and did not linger, we were told by the Prince, by the Church, to praise God. Further south, they said, in the Kingdom of Sicily, things were worse. So too was it further north. But in Verona we were blessed.

Blessed!

A curse upon that blessing.

I had no choice but to take refuge in the one place I had forsworn. No other would take me in. If I would but swear fealty, false though it might be, to the God who favored the Princes and Nobility of Verona, the God who spat upon the fortunes of my family, if I would but swear fealty to *him*, then they might take me in.

Thus I joined the Franciscans, becoming a Friar in their Order.

Years passed and time marched across my body and mind, and weary though both became, never did my spirit waver. I established myself as the benevolent Friar of Verona, a holy man with no allegiance who sought to provide spiritual balm to any who sought his guidance. In many things did I counsel Verona's new Prince, the boy Escalus. And I ingratiated myself with Houses Capulet and Montague. I puttered about in my garden, studying my herbs and nurturing growth and life in a town of death and rot. Blooms of ruby and sapphire containing precious ichor, weeds of unassuming appearance containing powers of life and death—these things I cultivated with no interference. So did I enter my five-and-twentieth year.

I could, I suppose, have let go of the thirst that consumed me.

Yet my dreams were filled with death—seeing my father trampled, of seeing the old Prince's indifferent face as the light of the rose window struck him, a holy mockery. Unholy fool! I would wake and rise and stalk the cloisters of the abbey, my eyes darting this way and that, seeing things unseen by day, shadows which moved and writhed before my sight. The shadows did not always talk, but they always reminded me of what I had lost.

Shuffling through the cold, stone halls, I held to my contempt.

And the plan began to form.

Even now, as you, one or both, read this, 'Lords' Capulet and Montague, you cannot guess of the depths—yes, the depths!—to which I was willing to plunge myself. The nighttime walks were lonely, isolating, and made me feel as though I was the last man upon the earth, a pathetic soul with only my memories and the shades of my dead and rotting family to accompany me from one dark corridor to the next.

I wandered—yes—I wandered! Aimless.

But not without result. For these walks caused me to ruminate, to enter deep reveries in search of some plan, some manner by which I might destroy Capulet, Montague, and all of Verona if I could.

It was upon one night, when my sanity mingled with the shadows and threatened to flee to that bitter country whence no man returns, that I remembered the legends. These ancient stories predate not only Rome, but even the Etruscans and those nameless peoples who came before them.

The Others.

Laugh, yes, laugh at me! Bellow through your tears and mock the man who has wrought death upon your Houses. I speak of the Others and you mock me, but know this: through powers beyond ancient have I visited tragedy upon you both. It is I who mock you, pathetic Capulet, and you, wretched Montague.

I studied the parchments and the histories we had in the abbey. For a long time, I feared that I had only imagined the Others. I thought perhaps my distempered brain had made them up, else pulled them from the collective memory of man. Yet the further I dug into our archives, the more hours I spent alone and shunning all but the most necessary company, the nearer I came to an answer: some origin for these whispered legends of things which lived in the woods.

At about this time, a young Romeo Montague came to the cathedral for spiritual guidance.

Perhaps twelve, not a hair above his lips nor the depth of a man's voice, Romeo was tractable, and so I became the kindly young Friar to him; his dear Friar Laurence, the man who provided him with spiritual succor and advice on life. The man he came to look upon as an older brother, almost.

Had he not possessed the arrogance of his father, I might have wavered in my goal.

But no.

I remained strong.

Is there any confection so sweet as irony? For it was Romeo who eventually placed his hands upon the volume I had been seeking. It was a summer of unprecedented heat. Flowers wilted, and green vines dried overhead in the gardens. Most of Verona, those who had the privilege at least, stayed indoors. Romeo was, as he made his habit in those days, with me in the libraries of the abbey. He did not know what I was seeking, and I did not tell him. I only asked him to look for volumes with specific words, both in Latin and other tongues, and eventually he found the book I sought.

Of course, I did not know at the time it was that which I needed. I shooed him away as might an indulgent older brother, and I began to read.

Let me tell you of them, the things older than the dirt under which your Romeo and your Juliet are buried.

Long before Verona was *Verona* as we know it, before the Romans were an empire, this land was lush, its forests heavy and dark. About the time of the construction of the Ponte Pietra over the Adige River, men told of spirits living in the woods. Before that, the Roman Consul, Spurius Magnus, records in his journal that construction on Via Postumia was briefly interrupted by the discovery of artifacts of unknown and ancient origin. While the road was being built, workers discovered shards of pottery and glass in the area surrounding what would become Verona. These shards depicted 'abominations' that Consul Magnus refused to elaborate on, other than to say that the creatures were 'pale' and 'wicked.'

Nothing is reported on what became of these artifacts, but I suppose that they were destroyed or lost in the nearly fifteen centuries that have passed since their discovery.

But I had it! Proof that the oldest legends of Verona had some basis in reality. It was even better for me that the Consul reported a few disappearances during the construction of that Roman road, and of men gone mad after sojourning in the woods alone. The men returned, babbling wildly of pale horrors that flitted out of sight in shaded glades, of ancient melodies, of blasphemies whispered into their ears.

These Others, these things predating Rome and Christ and everything that modernity considered 'civilized,' were the key.

No longer were my nightly wanderings filled with anguish. No more did the shadows follow me, for I now had a path upon which to walk toward a certain destination.

The only obstacle was Romeo Montague.

※

Indulge me if you will. Not that you have a choice. You have lost *everything*, and Verona is consumed by the flames of Hell. But if one thing tarnishes my soul in all this, if one person might have put all my plans to ruination, it was Romeo.

He was good.

Haughty, yes, like his family. But he possessed a curiosity about the world that was wasted upon someone in his position. In another life, perhaps he will be a great man—perhaps he will author great works or make a discovery on the natural order of things. For if the soul is reborn, as I think it might be, Romeo will surely be reborn into a time and place befitting his curiosity, his knowledge.

Despite my best efforts, he and I formed a friendship. As he grew from a little thing of twelve to a young man of fourteen, and then fifteen, and finally a tall, handsome youth of sixteen, so did his mind develop and his kindness flourish. These were tempered somewhat by his rashness, his passion for young women, and that Montague arrogance, yes; but a fairer person I never knew from those families. And a fairness that hid, for once, nothing.

What is goodness? What is evil? Does one evil action an evil person make? Can a good person do a wicked, even abominable, thing for a good reason? A noble one? What is a human but the sum of their parts? Can one person be defined by one action, or must they be weighed from a totality of their actions and set against the circumstances that a capricious God puts before them?

There is no clear answer, despite the Church saying there is—at least, I have not stumbled upon one. All my life, I have striven toward goodness despite my circumstances. I have exhibited Christian charity despite no belief in that God whom I cursed. I did what I could for a family that ultimately died despite my efforts. Yet I also contemplated and executed a plan of limitless depravity, and I feel no guilt for it.

Blood stains my hands, yet the spot of it does not bother me, does not wake me at night. Do my actions balance? Must I spend the remainder of my life doing good for others so as to cleanse what little stain remains upon my palm? If the spot remains and does not trouble me, does this mean my soul is unstained, or that I have grown cold and indifferent to anything which may stain it? Should the spot disappear and wash clean with the waters of time, does that mean that my guilt is also gone, or that the great cosmic *beyond*, whatever force it is that guides our lives, has absolved me?

As for the nobility of these deeds: what if they procure justice? Or, at the very least, a balancing of the scales? This world proclaims itself to be just, but such is only the case for those with the power and money to force it. For the rest of us, I say this: if justice be withheld from us, should we not bloody our hands to take it?

What of Romeo Montague? A boy who performed good actions, was an attentive friend, yet who also belonged to a family whose actions stain the streets of Verona. Let us not forget that he spilled the blood of Tybalt, Lady Capulet's beast of a nephew, and of Count Paris. Though Tybalt killed Mercutio and was not an innocent, and Count Paris was, like his kinsman the Prince of Verona, just as foul a vermin that ever infected our streets. Did their deaths stain Romeo's hands?

Know only that I, Friar Laurence Caroto, carry no guilt for what I have done.

In the weeks following Romeo's sixteenth birthday, I began to bring about my plan. I took walks in nature at any and all hours; none of the other Friars bore any suspicion over these wanderings. So it was that I went beyond the gates of Verona into those ancient woods one evening. I left the cloister as the sun began its descent, and by the time I reached the forests, I bathed in the dimness of the red, gloaming hour.

The trees were still, though a light breeze danced between the limbs. Great bursts of wildflowers dotted the gaps between the trees. White flowers hung in clusters overhead, and the sweet scent of something old filled the air.

I carried a basket in one arm, filled with gardening shears and a few linens, as it was always expected that I would bring back flowers from the wild. But these shears were sharper than ordinary. For, by reading as much of the ancient texts as I could find in the years leading to this moment, I knew that blood was required.

I stood before a thicket of flowers of every color: yellow spring roses, pink lady slippers, creamy blue foxgloves—all manner of beautiful delights. Some, like the foxglove, held exquisite death within their juices.

Taking the shears, I pierced my thumb and squeezed drops of blood upon one of the flowers.

"By this pricking of my thumb," I said, "ancient beings my way come. And should I speak these words aright, come to me, merry wand'rer of night."

More blood I squeezed out upon the flower which holds death in its petals.

And I waited.

Three times I repeated the incantation, and three times I offered blood upon the foxglove. When the moon had risen and bathed me in its lonely, silver glow, I heard something from the thickets beyond. I turned, narrowing my eyes, and beckoned what had come to make itself known, that I may glimpse upon it.

Something crawled amongst the flowers. It pulled itself up, and I imagined some rough beast that would bring me closer to this reckoning, that would reveal to me how to bring the great calamity upon *your* Houses.

It rose, a creature so pale and white that it could be made of marble. Slender fingers beckoned me, and eyes pitiless and black as the void of night gazed upon me. I stood and faced the thing with the might of my will. The Other was older than perhaps all the legends of man combined; it was the face of a nightmare, the origin of all demoniacal lore and mythology, the source of all angelic and ethereal beauty that we think of as confined to dreams. Perchance a source of both dreams and nightmares, agony and ecstasy, it was a thing that had been with us since the beginning of time.

As I yearned to flee, so did my passions arise. I longed to caress the divine face, to press myself against his solid frame. As he—yes, it was a *he*—stepped into the silver light, my passions grew and my face flushed. I wanted to know him, for him to know me, yet I wanted to run, to claw my eyes from my skull and to bash it against the nearest rock, spilling my brains upon the grass. We were never meant to see these Others. I felt rage and sorrow at my grief; joy and rapture at the idea of vengeance; fear of being in the presence of something so old; and lust for its lithe, masculine body.

"Laurence of Verona," he said.

I found my voice, though it quavered. "What is your name, wanderer of the night? For names are power, and if you have mine, then I must have yours."

He stepped fully from the grove of flowers. He was my height, though I felt like an insect beside him. He trailed his fingers along tree bark, and where they touched, white petals bloomed before falling to the grass.

"My truest name you could utter not, for your tongue would spasm, twist, and rot. Yet for you, dear Friar, I shall tell you this: my name on this plane, though sealed with a kiss."

"Yes," I said, swallowing. And so he stepped up to me, his hard body against me, his pearl-white lips open, and he pressed them against mine. Though I am a young man still in the scheme of things, this act I could not tell anyone; yet oh, such joy I derived from those forbidden lips. I kissed the fair Other who came from the twisted roots of the earth upon my beckoning. He took my breath and gave it back. I wanted more of him even as he pulled away.

"And now," he said, "your soul is mine should you spill my name upon this earth. Should you so much as write it down, your death would be my mirth."

"Speak no more in rhyme," I said. "Deal with me plainly. I am owed that much."

"Be it well," the fair Other said. "My name is Robin Goodfellow, elsewise known as the sweet hobgoblin, Puck." Neither of these were his true name, nor are they approximations, but for the purposes of this I shall use them—for they came to my mind as I wrote this, guided, even, by hands unseen.

"You want something from me," he said. "This much I know. Something *dreadful*. Lucky you, that I answered your call. There are few of us left, some more ill-tempered than others. Fewer still are the humans who know how to gain an audience with us. My congratulations. Now, if what you want from me be truly wicked, the product of an abandoned and malignant heart, and better still, if it brings misery to others, something succulent that I may enjoy, then I am at your service. For I love a good trick or two."

"Then we have common ground," I said. I began to outline to him my plan. What I wanted, namely the destruction of Capulet and Montague—all of Verona, if it could be managed. But if not, the lives of those who had wronged me would do. The scheme I had in mind was something that I had worked on for years in my head, though dared not write down. Yet I recited it with ease to this merry Puck, whose dark eyes gleamed and white teeth glistened the more I explained.

"And is there a maiden daughter of Lord Capulet?"

"Yes," I said, "her name is Juliet."

He grinned. "Then it must come to pass that the two of them meet and fall in love."

"Would it were that easy," I said, "for Romeo has, these past few weeks, been enamored of one of Capulet's nieces, Rosaline. Whether she returns the affection I do not know, but to wound the families fatally, I must strike at their hearts—and that means Juliet. Though Romeo changes his lovers as much as the moon changes its face, if not more."

"Then what you need," the creature said, "is a bit of holy ichor."

In his bone-white hand he produced a vial, empty but filled with possibility. He plucked a white petal from the branch above, squeezed its juice into the glass, discarding the petal. From a purple foxglove, stained still with my blood, he squeezed more liquid. At last, merry Puck spit into the mixture and flicked it with a finger, swirling it—and handed me the elixir.

"Have you access to Juliet?"

"She and her family pray at the cathedral abutting my abbey," I said. "She often seeks my counsel."

"Then take a hair of hers," Puck said, "drop it in this vial. Then this—it is the important part! Having this juice, you must watch Romeo when he is asleep, and drop the liquor of this vial into his eyes—the next time he lays eyes upon Juliet, be his mood foul or fair—he shall pursue her with the soul of love, for in love's depths shall his soul be lost. And as for her, leave that to me."

"And," I said, "should I contrive for them to meet, the rest will be in my hands. The plan has been long, but I am sure of it."

"Strike without mercy or hesitation," said the merry Puck, "and your aim will not miss. Oh, how delicious the chaos will be, and the pain."

I smiled. "Violent delights have violent ends. In my triumph they die, in my kiss do they perish."

For a second, the forest was quiet. All the natural wildlife had fled in the presence of the being standing before me, naked and lithe, marblelike in his stature. I held the vial, felt the ecstasy of vengeance flow through my blood, causing my wrists to pulse, trilling up my arm like ardent desire.

"I am glad I answered the blood-borne call," Puck said. "This will be violent fun. And you, my handsome young friar: I would crown you with flowers and make myself all of your joy for the rest of your days. For you, I would put a girdle around the earth in forty seconds; for you I would shatter the walls of Verona, of the ancient Jericho, of cities whose names have been blasted to dust by history's whims. If you would but allow me this, I swear—as I am an honest Puck—I swear I shall be at your service and carry out beautiful, merciless death upon Verona. We shall soak the earth with their blood. I shall make you the arbiter of all Verona's fate. If you would allow me to remain with you, to show you the garden of earthly delights, to keep you as mine and myself as yours when our work is done."

If there is a Christian devil, he knows not the tenth of the blasphemies of that jolly Puck, and of the fair folk who creep in the woods beyond Verona. If there is a Devil, let his blood run cold with the pact I made that night. Let him turn his face away from the suffering I have wrought. Let him tremble before the power of a force beyond his reckoning.

Let him pity you Capulets and Montagues, for in me, there is none.

The course of true love never did run smooth, but coarser paths drive love toward tragedy. This is truer still when mine is the hand which guides the journey. Some say that journeys end in lovers meeting. Perhaps it is best to say that, in Verona, a meeting of lovers does lovers' lives end.

As I had predicted, a contingent of Capulet 'ladies' attended prayers at the cathedral. Juliet, with her little face framed in soft, honeyed hair, prayed with all the duty expected of the daughter of Lord Capulet. Kneeling before the altar, her blue silk dress spreading like water across the stone floor, she was a vision of pious wealth. Her nurse was with the girl the whole time.

I took my chance.

"Madame," I said, "if I may, there is a burr upon your shoulder—such an abhorrent thing, though from nature it might be, belongs not on the garment of an angel divine." I had a burr palmed and at the ready; I reached for the girl's shoulder, where there lay several strands of loose hair. Using the burr, I snagged the few fallen wisps, held them my palm and showed her and the nurse the burr.

"Thank you, good Friar," Juliet said. She stood, nodded to me, and left, attended by her nurse and a maid.

From there, it was as though the fates guided my path. An easier job I could not have asked for. Romeo came one day to my cell as I worked upon the herbs from my garden.

"If you come more often still," I said with an indulging smile, "Lord Montague might think it is a monk you wish to be—and does not fair Romeo carry the weight of his family name?"

The boy collapsed into the chair reserved for visitors. "A monk! Oh, if only a monk I could be, that I might have sweet rest from love's unrelenting spell."

"Ah," I said, "so then Rosaline continues to haunt your dreams?"

"Yes, though haunt me less she might, if a look of love she would give in turn. Though Lord Capulet has a daughter. As does Lord Caligari! Lords and their daughters, they vex one so, do they not?"

And so I learned that he already had laid eyes upon Juliet. A single push, a nudge in the right direction—was this all I needed?

I sat with him and sighed, bemoaned the troubles of the heart. A good Friar I am, an honest Laurence, and so I offered him tea that might calm his nerves, and he drank as he read. He drank more still, and then his eyes drooped and his head lolled back. Did you know how softly your boy snored, Lord Montague? Know you how human and vulnerable he was in that moment, when I dripped into his eyes the ichor of those enchanted, midsummer woods mingled with Juliet's hair?

He slept some while still, and not till the sun in its red-glow waning did he wake. Shafts of light struck his innocent face, and I gently admonished him for sleeping.

"I am the youngest Brother in these cloisters," I said. "I am used to old men sleeping, but not youths! Surely your heart cannot be that worn out by love for Rosaline?"

"If she only gave me a look," he said with a yawn, "a sign, a little something, I might be able to sleep at night. I know I ought to do more, Father Laurence, and live by the day and stalk not the corridors of my mind at night—I've heard all the admonishments! Cousin Benvolio and friend Mercutio have tried persuading me into nonsense like sneaking into balls and running the streets. But it matters not, if Rosaline will not be mine."

"Now, what's this about sneaking into a ball?"

Lord Capulet, it seemed, was holding a ball. The youths planned on sneaking in, though to what purpose I could not discern. From the sound of it, the thing would be pure decadence. I suppressed an angry frown at the thought of the wealthy who trample the streets of Verona by day, partying by night, not at all concerned with the lives of those they ruin.

"You should not sneak into a Capulet event," I said. "However…Is Rosaline to be at this ball? Lord Capulet's daughter she might not be, but surely a niece would attend—but no, ignore my ramblings. Whether Rosaline is at the ball or not, it is no concern of *mine*."

Within the boy's eyes new fire flickered to rosy life.

Again I ask whether man serves himself, or whether he serves the whims of a fate he cannot see. True, I employed the use of merry Puck's liquor to enflame the passions of young Romeo, and Puck worked his own invisible mischief. Truer still that I helped plant the seed in Romeo's mind to attend Lord Capulet's affair so that he might see Rosaline. Yet he was already developing eyes for Juliet, and his friends Benvolio and Mercutio were already trying to persuade him to attend the ball. Better still, on the day following my conversation with Romeo, a street fight between the Capulets and Montagues resulted in the vermin Prince declaring that another outburst would result in the death of the perpetrator. Tighter did the screw turn, by my actions and those beyond my control.

Human society is a tempest which tosses each individual to and fro. In great masses do we move in crashing waves. The tides of history and political action are beyond us. How much control we have over where the storm takes us as individuals, I do not know. Perhaps things in Verona were always headed this way. Perhaps I was merely a puppet of the fates.

A happier one they could not have chosen.

Some few days after these events, a wistful Romeo wandered into the garden as I snipped the leaves from an oleander. The spicy scent of its poison blood filled my lungs, and I thought fondly of Puck, watching, perhaps, from some perch in the woods. He promised to watch events unfold, and I hoped he was watching now.

Romeo waved to me. His grin was dreamy.

"Good morrow, Father!"

I stood. It was early, very early. The sun had only just risen. Romeo had not been in bed the previous night; I could see the exhaustion in his eyes. Yet, there too was the flame which had sparked days ago, now a roaring inferno. I chided him for having spent the evening with Rosaline.

"Rosaline! What name is Rosaline to me?" he asked, kicking at a few weeds with the toe of his shoe. "That name was once sweet but has now soured on my tongue. No, no, it isn't Rosaline—why could it be her? How? How could my heart belong to Rosaline when there is a fairer beauty for my heart?"

"Oh, stop prattling," I said. "Tell me what you mean."

The trap had worked. Juliet now had his heart. I always knew there was some risk, some chance that she might not return his love. She was a silly goose, though, with no knowledge of the world or its bitter taste, and Romeo was a handsome youth with insatiable love for her. What girl could resist that? Were they always destined to fall so strongly toward each other? Was it Puck's doing?

"You must marry us today," Romeo said.

I feigned shock chided him. As the sun rose and warmed the garden I reasoned with him, knowing that he was beyond any sense that he possessed, until finally I relented, under the ostensible hope that a marriage would unite the families.

We set the wedding for the morrow, and I sent little messengers here and there to arrange the affair so that it might come off perfectly. I, a holy man, with eyes only for uniting two houses and ending the conflict of Verona, possessed no outward sign of guilt. My every action bespoke that altruistic desire to see peace come to Verona.

That night I took another walk to the woods, and there I suggested to Puck, who sat in the whispering trees, that someone might whisper into Tybalt's ear. His blood was near the boil, my little messengers told me, from Romeo slipping into the Capulet ball. Another whisper, be in his dreams or on the street, would push him further toward—well, any manner of things.

"And so," Puck said as we stood beneath the falling petals in a moonlit clearing, "more players enter the game, and more blood may soak the streets. Leave the whispering to me. My poison tongue shall finish fate's work. Worry no more about Tybalt."

So I worried not. Instead I lifted a warm hand to his stony cheek, brushed him with my fingers. His floral breath mingled with mine.

"If you and I are to be each other's after the mischief is done," I said, "I would almost have it done now."

His eyes grew soft, as did his bloodlust grin.

Puck said, "With more players in the game, and higher risks, perhaps it be better if we were to seal the agreement anew, and with more vigor."

I agreed. Sealing the new terms of the plan was ecstasy.

TO MAKE THE DEVIL'S BLOOD RUN COLD

What is the point, Capulet and Montague, of regaling you with everything that happened thereafter? Know that I married your son and your daughter in secret, knowing full well that the bliss would never last, that their joy would bear the weight of corruption until it and their lives collapsed. All I can say is that, while I had the end in mind—a total destruction of your families, everything hinged upon precise timing and boiling tempers. Whether I pushed the tempest in one direction, or whether it moved where it was always going to crash, it matters not.

Tybalt challenges Romeo to a duel. Romeo declines. Mercutio picks up the sword in his stead and is mortally wounded. Places a curse upon Houses Capulet and Montague. Romeo, the rash fool that he is, slays Tybalt. This you know.

But oh, how the ruby liquid seeped into the yellow stones of Verona under the pitiless sun! I watched, yes, and savored every moment. Such blood that day, in the fountains!

Oh, how quickly things fall apart.

Romeo—exiled under penalty of death! Even a week before the events, I might have inwardly wept for what I must do to the boy who had shown me no personal harm. Yet the shadows of my family that ever crept in the corners of my cell, their eyes that peered from between leafy garden overgrowth, would not leave me be. I promised them that I would remain strong, and so I deadened my heart.

Juliet—betrothed to Count Paris! She and Romeo, consummating their damnation. Tighter still wound the spring.

With Romeo banished I knew the time was set for the final act—a suggestion to Juliet that a little tincture to give her the pallor of death, to secure her a spot in the family tomb, where she could await, awake, and be reunited with Romeo. The little thing trusted me, and for a moment I thought to simply poison her and be done with it. But no—for the fullness of the plan the two must murder themselves. So I gave her the tincture—yes, Lord Capulet, it was I who did that—could you but doubt it at this point in the narrative?

I promised her I would send a letter to Romeo explaining the plan.

I did not promise the letter would arrive on time. Selecting the sickliest messenger I could find and the very last hour at which a letter could duly arrive, did the trick nicely.

From the cold crypt I watched, waiting hour after bated hour till the minute Paris and Romeo met in the churchyard gloom. Knowing well the crypt and its layout, I knew where to stand for the best view of their battle. Never did I doubt Romeo would prevail, and win he did. Another sinner of Verona down, more blood soaking the earth.

As Romeo, the boy become man, walked into the crypt, I let myself drift to the shadows. He carried the body of slain Paris, whose slender fingers dripped ruby rain onto the gray stone. With cold evening light framing them, it occurred to me that this was always going to come to pass. Whether I was irrelevant to the turning of the wheel of fortune, or whether I was a necessary instrument of it, I still do not know. But the unconscious girl, the dead Count, the grieving youth—they made a portrait of fate with I the viewer. It could not have happened precisely so without me; I was a tool, discardable, replaceable—yet essential still.

However works the stage of history, I played my bloody part with relish.

Mewling, pathetic boy! He laid Paris upon the ground, stood and swept his hands over Juliet's visage, tucked a lock of her hair behind her ear. He prattled on, and I worried he would speak long enough that he might see her revive—my heart thrashed in its mortal cage, and I waited for him to turn his dagger against himself.

How easily I could have stepped from the shadows and cleared the matter up.

Ultimately he took a vial from his pocket, some poison I know now, and drank it to the last drop.

"Thus with a kiss, I die."

These were his final words, Lord Montague. From the time I first met Romeo till I watched the soul flee his eyes and the foam gather on his rosy lips, he was a good boy. So too was my father a good man. Such is life, Montague.

And Capulet! As to your daughter—I left the crypt and the churchyard unseen, then 'came upon' the ordeal a half-hour later. I regret that I could not watch Juliet kill herself, as she revived in time to shoo me

TO MAKE THE DEVIL'S BLOOD RUN COLD

away (and I had yet my part to play as the innocent), but we know how it all turned out. Her happy dagger finished what I started.

If I could, I would spend a hundred pages telling you, Capulet and Montague, of the delight it brought me to watch your grief. To inwardly howl with triumph as I gave you my version of events, my *piety* as you proclaimed me to be 'a holy man.' All evidence proved my testimony true—as it undoubtedly would—and I was prepared for the bloodiest war which Verona has seen.

And yet you two made peace!

Peace, after all my efforts! I could not allow it. And so let me tell you, now that it is done, my final act.

Your ladies made a sorry sight as they came to the newly christened crypt of Juliet and her Romeo. Nearly bosom friends! Their tears seemed to be forging a new friendship—for this I had not planned. No! I could not tolerate it, could not permit the work of fate to go so far only to whimper out in pathetic gestures of friendship. But the friendship was fragile yet, and easily shattered.

I made one final tincture, this one of the oleander plant which I have cultivated so carefully. Distilled into absolute lethality.

What if, I asked myself, the two Highborn women of Houses Capulet and Montague tried to pay respects to their children as a pair, and, instead of coming together in their grief, began to blame one another for their family's ills? What if one took up the very dagger with which Juliet had ended her life and plunged it into the heart of the other? What if the gruesome scene were all arranged just so, to leave no doubt in the minds of the broken fathers and husbands that their women had attacked one another? What havoc might be caused if the bloody feud were not dimmed by the death of innocence, but rather brought to unstoppable fury?

Grieving mothers easily accept tea when offered by benevolent Friars. Odd that it may be for a Friar to offer tea at a family crypt, who asks questions of one known by all to be a holy man?

"We thank you, Father," Lady Capulet said.

"For the tea, for the comfort, for the holy words," Lady Montague added.

The key, Lords Capulet and Montague, to staging a crime such as this, is to poison the mourners with a tea that takes its time. You must wait until that vital moment: when the one is collapsed, but her heart beating still, and the other similarly immobile. You must strike—and hard!—while the heart still pumps. You must ensure that it is Lady *Montague* you stab with the blade which brought Juliet her end. The blade you had to procure from offices that only the high and holy have access to—so that it would appear that Lady Capulet or her agents took the blade for vengeance.

When the one has bled out, you strangle the other.

In this way, it appears that the destruction was violent and mutual.

And you have the final spark required to set the two most powerful families against each other, so beset by grief, so utterly raw that they cannot think beyond the obvious.

In this way, a humble boy become Friar, Laurence Caroto, took the justice that Verona would not pay him.

I strolled the city streets shortly after the Prince's assassination. My merry Puck and I, hand in bloodied hand, strolled the old cobblestones as flames spilled from the Capulet manor, kissing the night sky and drowning the stars in unholy light. As we reached the square where Tybalt was slain, a maid from House Montague, sooty-faced and bleeding, approached me. She seemed not to see Puck as she knelt before me.

"Father," she cried, "mercy! Have mercy—they've killed us! They've—"

I kicked her in the face. I ruminated earlier in this narrative on whether the spots of blood might wash from my skin. Now I think them rather lovely stains.

"Laurence dearest," he said with his cunning grin. "You were made to live among us. Before Verona, there was a beautiful glade, and we were happy without the pall of mankind; yet we were driven from our home, confined to the woods. We deal not with humans, only when we must, but you, I think, might be welcomed in our unholy court."

I touched his cloud-white lips. "Have I yet made the Devil's blood run cold with what we have done? Would he fain beg the mercy of Heaven rather than look upon me?"

Puck smiled. "Oh, such fun we will have. I promised you a garden of earthly delights, but perhaps it is *you* who will show me things that even the wickedest heart dare not dream of." We stood on the steps of the Basilica di San Zeno Maggiore. There was a burst of flame and a golden glow as the church caught fire from within.

"Once, I thought what I would do, were the world mine," I told my Puck, "but the world is *ours*, and now—why wait for my tongue to catch your body's precious melody, for our bodies to be as one—why hold off on exquisite blasphemy? Be mine now, and I will be yours— here! In sight of the doors where once I begged for mercy and found none."

Puck drew a finger across my jaw and said, "Unholy man, I am yours to command."

Thus in ecstasy did we complete our journey, there upon the steps of the Basilica. And as we did, the rose window shattered inward with the heat of the fire consuming Verona.

And now I finish. By the time you read this I shall be among the Others, watching you all, no doubt, and sipping the nectar of your agony. But before I nail this narrative to the doors of every burnt-out church in this crumbling husk of a city, I say my last.

Capulet and Montague, know this:

Your holy man played you for unholy fools because you refused, years ago, to atone for your sins. Say what you will of me. I have rendered justice, yes. But in doing so, I have ascended to something beyond good and evil, beyond human—I have become the god of your destruction.

And so I shall be tomorrow, and tomorrow, and tomorrow still, and through all of time. I am the master of the stage upon which you perform your petty little tragedies, and it is I who shall sweep away all players, snuff you out like candles, should I desire.

Remember this.

MATHEW L REYES

For you are all the shadows of *nothing*.
Your being is nothing, signifying *nothing*.
And I am everything.

Signed,
   Frate Laurence Caroto di Verona

LEND ME THY HAND
(TITUS ANDRONICUS)
WILLIAM STEFFEN

The fire is roaring now. Bright and hot.

I remember the pie cooling on the sill. My hands in the leaves. Tree branches. Birch. Poplar. A river of blood in my throat. The Tiber. The Thames.

Now it is ink I dribble from my lips. I rose this morning not intending to become a historian by sundown; but now, how can I possibly be quiet? A lady does not need a tongue to speak, nor hands to write with. I have met my share of women who can do naught but wag with the one and quibble with the other. But I must be brief, else my head fall from my shoulders from too much dotting of my I's and gnashing at my T's. The quill my chin does steer bears a foul odor and, I can imagine, a still fouler taste. There are times, no doubt, it serves to want a tongue.

A hand on my throat. Tree branches. Poplar. My hands in the leaves. Oak. My hands in the earth.

Winter came to my father's estate this Hallowtide's eve in the form of two boys, whose names were of this morning only faintly familiar to me, and whose faces shall be but remembrances now. Dead are they, as doornails driven home.

I have had such trouble remembering things of late that it is all I can do to write them down. There are things I still cannot quite recall —the bloodstains in the marble hall seem familiar to me, but I do not remember how they got there. I do not know where my brothers are. What became of my mother? Or my tongue? My hands? I remember (now) how they were lost, but the hand of my father too? What stars or gods did my father cross to become so stricken with handlessness? When shall our suffering end, and what is it for? Father found me last week, praying before a portrait of my mother hanging in the temple. When I pressed him about her, he only howled and gnashed his teeth, then retreated into a corner of the house—the armory I think—where he licks his wounds and sharpens his daggers. He still has his tongue, you see.

But there are things I know now that I must not forget—the Tiber and the Thames. The river of blood. Tree branches. The smell of cinnamon and nutmeg. The sounds of applause. Hounds barking. Soul-cakes.

A cold wind blew from the North when I saw their carriage arrive by the East gate. The inkblot sky stood gray and still while curling fingernails of light drizzle tapped on my window. To the west, I watched the fiery gold leaves of my father's park drain of their color until that great gray patch of fog rolled in, obscuring my view and enveloping the estate.

From my writing desk, perched before my bedroom window, through the stained-glass panels depicting Philomena weaving a tapestry for Procne—is there no place I can escape the archetype of my disaster?—I heard the children squeal from the carriage, their mother squawking to control them. They threw their fists at one another until their noses bled and their crowns were cracked, then fell in laughing together, each brother's shoulder serving as his own. The boys were already in their costumes, pulling them from one another like cats in straw. The mother—the Queen, as Father calls her—wore an outfit as much like the night as her sons' were. I remember thinking —but how long ago this afternoon was! how much younger was I then! —that in outfits like those, the boys would surely disappear in the dead of night. Especially during souling.

LEND ME THY HAND

Kindling in my hands. A hole in the woods. A river of blood. The cry of hounds. A Moor.

I listened while the Queen made Father guess which mage or brine pit her complexion most resembled. He played along and promised to bring her boys to the feast after the souling.

"Don't worry, your Grace," my father told her. "Your boys are in good hands. Good hands."

I rolled my eyes.

I watched as the carriage rode away into the mist and continued writing. What came in only fragments then hath been remembered now. Trimmings of dialogue that were clipped before now stand firmly rooted in my memory. I must separate the lies from the truth, the blood from the water, the Thames from the Tiber. I remember the Queen's speech, which, hearing, made my hands turn into fists. I remember my hands before my uncle found them in the leaves.

No sooner had they told this hellish tale,
But straight they told me they would bind me here
Unto the body of a dismal yew,
And leave me to this miserable death:

I was dressed by the time the lock finally turned and my father darkened my doorway. He wore a chef's cap and an apron. I do not believe I've smiled these past twelve months but a handful of times—O! Woe is me! Albeit seeing my father in that outfit nearly made me weep with mirth.

"Soul, souls for a soul-cake," he whispered somberly. His utterance was too dark, indeed, for either one of us to keep from erupting in laughter. "Pray you, good mistress, a soul-cake!"

I gestured at him. I had no idea why he had chosen to play the cook.

"Tonight, my Lav," he said, stepping forward into the pale light of my bedchamber, "I am my daughter's chauffeur, chef, and company." His beard was ragged and his tears had cut deep rivers into his face. His voice was hoarse and small, as though he had been shouting to Olympus. "What about you? Are you going as a princess?"

I rolled my eyes at him.

"There, there. I know a princess when I see one. And I know a

Thracian princess when I see one of those too." He withdrew further into the shadows behind the doorway before he disappeared completely. I jotted down another phrase before descending after him:

And then they call'd me foul adulteress,
Lascivious Goth, and all the bitterest terms
That ever ear did hear to such effect:

Downstairs, the boys were fencing with the fire pokers by the massive hearth in the dining room. Screams and arguments echoed through the great rooms. The eyes of my fallen brethren, whose portraits lined the walls, stared at the adolescents with solemn indifference, or perhaps contempt.

"That's a hit!"

"Was not! No fair!"

"Take that!"

Father did not seem to mind how loud they were. He did not seem to regard them at all.

Your boys are in good hands.

He was in the kitchen, covered in flour. There was flour everywhere. It had fallen thickly onto the kitchen floor, where his heavy footsteps fumbled about. Some of the flour had made it into the pie dough, which Father was rolling out—quite clumsily—with his forearms and extant palm. I hugged a rolling pin from the counter and began to show him a better way.

"I don't recall asking for a hand," he said. "But if you wish to help, hand me the pie plates."

I embraced the stack of pie plates from the counter and began to spread them out. There were a dozen in all. But I did not any filling see.

"For the Hallowmas feast," my father said, addressing the questions furrowing in my brow. "A dozen pies for the Emperor and the Queen. But we can finish later. The sun is going down, and we do not want to be late for the souling." He beat his chest, the way I imagined he sometimes would in battle. A ghost of flour lifted from his apron and fell silently to the floor.

The hole in the woods. My hands in the leaves. Tree branches. Chiron and Demetrius. Mustn't forget.

LEND ME THY HAND

"Boys!" my father shouted. I know now that he would not speak their names. From the dining room, the fire pokers crashed to the floor and the boys came in. They would not look at me. Instead, they scooped flour from the floor and began throwing it at one another until their onyx habiliments were shrouded in white powder.

And, had you not by wondrous fortune come,
This vengeance on me they had executed.
Revenge it, as you love your mother's life,
Or be ye not henceforth call'd my children.

"Boys!" My father commanded the walls themselves with his voice. The boys stopped at once and looked at him. "The time has come." He handed them each a satchel. He gave one to me as well. "For the soul cakes," he said. "Follow me."

My father lit a lantern and hung it from his fingerless forearm. At the door, he put his hand on the latch, then stopped. He turned to look at me and the two boys. "Remember: stay together. Hallowmas is no time to go off wandering by oneself. There are goblins and ghouls about."

"I'm not afraid of goblins!" one of the boys contested.

"Yeah, me neither. Nor ghoul nor ghost neither," the other one said.

"Then you can lead the way, boys!"

Outside, the rain had stopped but the fog remained. It was a mile, at least, to the first neighbor, who lived at the edge of the park, and night had come in her sable robes by the time we reached it. Despite my father's warning, the boys ran ahead and kicked at the door. It creaked open and an old woman with biscuits stood silhouetted against the fire burning at her back.

"Soul, souls for a soul-cake!" The boys said, holding out their satchels. "Pray you, good mistress, a soul-cake!"

"It's about time you lot showed up," the woman said. "I was beginning to think we'd have to eat these cakes ourselves. And what might you pair be, then?"

Chiron—or was it Demetrius?—did not answer her, but snatched the cake from her hands and ran away. The other one uttered a foul word and skipped off into the darkness of his brother's shadow.

The old woman nearly shut the door entirely before she saw that there was one more souler.

"Oh aren't you lovely!" she said. "Take a few more steps my dear. Into the light, now. Don't be shy."

I looked back at my father, barely visible in the fog, his chef's cap and apron gleaming white in the swallowing gray. He stood in the road and urged me forward with his hand.

"And what might you—dear God! You poor thing!" The woman dropped the soul-cakes she was holding and nearly fell backwards. A man stepped into the doorway and caught her before she fell.

"Now Nell, what is it? You look as though you've seen a—great Jupiter!"

"You poor thing," the woman cried, finding her balance but keeping her distance. "What is it that has happened to ye?"

"Do you need help, young lass?" The man asked. "Are ye hurt?"

I crept toward them and tried to pick up the soul-cake from the mud where it had fallen, but it only crumbled into pieces in the ungentle hold between my arms.

"Are you a goddess, then?" The woman asked. "Is that what yer meant to be, dressed in white?"

"Ay, a goddess of hell, if I ever seen one," the man replied. "A harpy is more like it."

"Oh, shut up, Marcus," the woman said, pushing the man aside. "I apologize, deary. I didn't mean to give you such a fright. And there's no excuse for my husband."

"I think she's the one what ought to be apologizin' to you, isn't she?" Marcus said, as though my ears had been lopped off as well, and my hearing with them.

"Shut up, Marcus."

"I'm only sayin'. What an awful, pitiful sight. Who do you suppose would do something like that to someone?"

"Shut up, now, Marcus. I mean it."

"So do I. And why do you suppose her face is painted black like it is? Is that supposed to be a beard? Why girl, any soul with two eyes can see what a delicate creature you are. Or were, before—"

"Marcus, shut up!" The woman took three more soul-cakes from a bowl and timidly dropped them in my bag. I tried to say thank you, but the noise I made with my mouth only summoned fresh horror for the woman and more questions from the man. I hurried back into the fog to find my father.

We could hear the boys ahead of us, howling and summoning mischief. "Soul, souls for a soul-cake!" echoed strangely in the distance between peals of laughter, angry bouts of swearing, and the sound of glass breaking. Father seemed oblivious. He whistled a somber tune to himself that came to him from somewhere in the fog. He escorted me from one house to the next until my satchel was full of soul cakes. The neighbors seemed to grow less tolerant of my appearance as the evening wore on. One man told me I reminded him of a slave he had once and asked me if I had lost my hands for stealing from my master. Another man, shrinking with age and leaning on a cane, told me that my face reminded him of a Moor he knew once, and he wanted me to know how many friends of his were Moors. A boy said I reminded him of the puppets he saw at the Skimmington.

At the last house, a woman with a baby told me that two boys had just snatched all of her soul-cakes.

"Broke our window, too, didn't they, dear?"

The woman's husband gave me a fright. When he came to the door, I—I thought he was someone else. He stood silhouetted against the firelight, so I could not see his face. It was only once I saw that he was, in fact, afraid of me that I realized he could not have been the man I feared.

"Do...do you know those boys?" He asked from deep within the one-roomed house.

I neither nodded nor shook my head. I only held my swollen bag before me.

"My wife already told you those boys made off with the rest of our soul cakes. They also...they also tried to kidnap our boy from us."

Suddenly there was a hand upon my shoulder. "What is the trouble here, my girl?"

"Noble Titus!" the man said, stepping through the doorway and kneeling in reverence. "Forgive us. We did not mean to frighten the girl. We were only telling the princess of the two boys who were here.

They tried to take our babe, and when we wouldn't surrender him unto them, they threw rocks into our house and broke two of our windows."

Father raised his only hand. "The boys are not mine, but they do go with us and apprehend the spirit of this night. They are clothed in mischief, head to toe, and do intend toward every earthly sin and transgression. Tell me: do you know what purpose they had with your child?" The baby began to wail and the woman pressed it closer to her breast.

"They said that they would pay for the child now and would deliver us a child unto his likeness in a day or two. But they produced no money, and the only intent I could perceive was murder or mutilation."

"Muli!" his wife chastised him.

"Forgive me, noble Titus and gracious Lavinia," he said.

"I take no responsibility for their actions," Father said, "but I will see they feel the consequences of them. I will not pay for your windows, but I can promise that I will add it to the ledger of their crimes. And when you feel the icy chill blow through your home, I hope that you will think of me and mine, and our estate that has grown lopped and lamed of late."

We circled back to the East gate. At the threshold, my father stopped. He told me he had to go and find the boys, but that I should go ahead and wait for him in the kitchen.

"We will make the pies," he said, "and then attend the Emperor's costume party with our pies in tow." I could see the house, but I did not want to leave my father.

"Go on, dear. I will be right behind you. I promise."

I started for the door. But only a few steps into my journey, I felt a chill run down my spine. I turned to find my father, but he was nowhere to be seen. I wanted to call out to him, but I was suddenly aware of how much fog there was and how those boys could have been anywhere. I dropped my satchel and made a dead sprint toward the house. Inside, it occurred to me that the boys could have come back early, that they might still be in the house. I ran to the dining room and wrestled to pick up the errant fire poker, lying cold and still on the great stone floor. The fire in the dining room was out; the fireplace was dark. The eyes of my brothers fell onto me from their perches on

LEND ME THY HAND

the wall. Quietly, I backed into the fireplace and crouched in the shadows.

In the dark I tried to remember. Tree branches. A pit. My brothers.

I awoke to the sound of my father whistling in the kitchen. The pies were in the oven and the smell was enchanting. My father's hand, nutmegged and be-cinnamoned, pounded dough on the countertop, tore it into strips, and wove it into a lattice. His apron was covered in cherry juice, and there were two tremendous burlap sacks leaning ponderously beside the kitchen hearth.

"Ah, my dear! I was wondering when you would be about." He tossed my satchel onto the counter, which was brimming over with soul-cakes now. "I found this outside. I think you may have dropped it."

"Did you find the boys?" I wanted to ask him. Instead, I dropped the fire poker.

"Ah, the boys. I'm sure they'll turn up. They'll turn up when they're good and ready. Right now, we need to get these pies made for the banquet. Give me a hand?"

I remember the pie cooling on the sill.

When we left, there was still no sign of the boys. Only the two burlap sacks and the extra soul-cakes in my satchel. And after all that, we only took one pie with us.

"It will be enough," my father told me in the carriage. A long silence fell between us. Then my father broke it.

"I have a thing to say," he said. And just when I thought he had finished his thought, he added, "I believe you. I didn't before. But I do now."

I glanced at him with a tilted head and a furrowed brow. Believe me? I did not know what he meant.

"You will know soon enough," he said, peeking out of the carriage. "You will be remembered."

And the next thing I knew, we were arriving and there were people in costumes everywhere. People wearing masks. Dressed as animals.

"Ah, you've arrived!" The Queen called out to us from across a crowded hall. "The ornament of Rome has arrived."

I remember tree branches.

After Father had presented his gift and explained his outfit through a smile that could cut glass, he handed the pie to me. The Queen pointed to the banquet table across at the other end of the room. I pushed my way into the crowd, past men in robes with faces like cats, past women in brightly-colored dresses with whiskers and mustaches. Women dressed as Diana, hunting in the woods. Men dressed as dogs, crawling for food on the floor. Dido and Aeneas, at home in Carthage. One man grabbed my arm. "Well, well, well," he said, but I tore free from his grasp and when I did, I saw that his black skin was only painted on and I wore his handprint on my elbow for the duration of the evening. I pushed through the crowd and when I reached the banquet at the end I found a table piled high with sweetmeats, with summer fruits somehow preserved and in season, with goblets full of wine. I found a place for the pie and set it down when I was overcome by the strangest sensation that someone was watching me. I turned and scanned the sea of faces, hidden by pasteboard masks, whispering to one another. They were all looking at me. How could they help themselves? Feast your eyes. It felt as though a ghost were breathing down my neck, holding a knife to my throat, daring me to turn around.

"Lav, darling, you look simply divine in those robes!" the Queen testified. "But what have you gotten all over your chin?" She dipped her fingers in the wine and began to rub the ink from my face. "There. That's gotten it."

My eyes were still fixed on the crowd when the Queen began to cut into the pie. "I'm simply famished. I'm delighted that your father baked pie! But do you know what kind? I suppose it doesn't matter."

She savored the first bite, like she was being restored. She swallowed the second one whole without even chewing. Then the third.

"I want you to know something," she said between mouthfuls, gristle dripping down her chin. "I want you to know that I admire how you have borne all of this." She waved her fork in my direction. "In a way, I have been where you have been. You are not a mother yet, but if you are ever blessed with children—if it is ever your misfortune to watch them slain before your very eyes and hacked to pieces—then you might know how willingly I would offer up my thumbs, feet, hands, fists, tongue—I would give up all of it to have my son back."

She put her hand on her stomach, the way pregnant women sometimes do. She shot a glance across the room at the Emperor. "I also know what it is to speak and to have no one heed your tongue. To be silenced. Even as a Queen, a woman is ever a plaything for men. Your father taught me that—what it means to be a slave. When he still had his faculties about him, I mean. Before he became this dithering old fool who, though he once led armies and commanded camps, now bakes pies and babysits children."

I did not need to defend my father from such slander. I knew the truth. I had seen my father crying in his armory, laughing in his misery, sticking needles in his thighs and conversing with the gods. He was not a man to be trifled with. Nor underestimated.

"Oh, darling!" she continued. "I almost forgot to ask! Where are the boys? Did they return with you?"

I did not meet her gaze. I have learned from experience that if you simply ignore people for long enough—or if you let them look at you until they become bored with jeering or else so sick they vomit—they will leave you alone. I said nothing.

"Oh forget it," she said with a smile. "I'll go and ask your drooling father."

When she left me, I felt the chill on the back of my neck again, like the cold breath of the dead. I turned, and there he was. The face. The eyes. The regal disposition preserved in a painted tapestry hung above the table. Our host's dear brother, and my betrothed. My deceased.

Bassianus.

Suddenly, I remembered everything—I was whole again. There were no more gaps in my memory. I remembered it all. It all came back to me with the force of the Tiber and the Thames. The hand on my neck. The hole in the woods. My dear husband's face. Hounds barking in the distance. The pillow. The trunk. My hands in the leaves. Tree branches. A dagger in my mouth. A river of blood. Chiron. The Tiber. Demetrius. The Thames. Tamora. The yew tree. Aaron. The baby. My father's hand. My brothers' heads. Everything. It was all I could do to scream.

They were all of them looking at me now, but not one of them showed the least bit of concern. That's just Lavinia, Titus's only daughter, who lost her hands and her tongue, who lost her brothers and her husband. She just does that now—screams from time to time when she bothers to remember. Stays pretty quiet the rest of the time.

The room was silent the moment I finally gasped for breath, preparing to scream again, but the Queen was screaming too now. It took me a moment to realize it was not in despair but in mockery —of me!

"Boo hoo! Has Rome forgotten about poor Lavinia Andronicus again?"

"Not Lavinia!" my father interjected with his commanding voice. "On the contrary, Rome hath not forgotten her most precious daughter, but her newest sons. Where are your boys, dear Queen?"

The Queen looked cornered at first, but her frown gently curled into a smile. "Oh, dear Titus. Have you forgotten? I left them with you. Or rather, I left you with them, you poor defenseless man."

"Wrong!" Father declared. "I'll ask you again. Where are your boys, Tamora?"

Her smile began to melt and her eyes darted around the hall.

"Chiron? Demetrius? I'm sure their disguises will keep them hidden until—"

"Wrong!" Father interjected again. "Hidden, they are not, your Grace. They are in plain sight—like their crimes. Behold, my daughter, by your lusty children cropped!"

"Titus!" Saturninus attempted to interject. "Enough!"

"Like the foul crimes of your associate the Moor, who took from me the heads of mine two sons, my hand—"

"Titus!" Saturninus said again. "Peace!"

"Your boys are in plain sight, Tamora my dear! As plain as the foul issue of thy illicit pregnancy, your Grace."

The Emperor looked at his wife, weighing the accusation. The Queen stood frozen, unable to move or even breathe. "Titus," she whispered through the silent room, "where are my—"

"Why, there they are both," he shouted, pointing to her bowels, "baked in that pie; whereof their mother daintily hath fed, eating the flesh that she herself hath bred. 'Tis true, 'tis true!"

LEND ME THY HAND

Tamora vomited in horror and collapsed onto the floor.

What happened next is still a blur, but it must be remembered here, however fragmented. My father stole a great cleaver from the banquet table with his one great hand and marched over to the woman puddled in her own filth upon the floor. As he raised his hand, the Emperor came from behind and lopped it from his wrist to spare his adulterous Queen. My father shrieked, and the knife fell from his arm with his hand still clutched around it. The blade glided to the floor and nicked the Queen's fair neck before it crashed and clamored on the ground. As blood flowed from her neck, Saturninus drove his saber through my father's chest and ended all his misery. It was a merciful gesture.

My uncle Lucius in turn slew the Emperor from behind with a saber all his own. The Queen writhed and choked, and then lay still beside her husband and my father.

My uncle brought me home. The house was freezing; I built a fire in the dining room. It is burning still, bright and hot as ever.

My father's pies were still upon the counter in the kitchen, beside the satchel with the soul cakes. I didn't realize how hungry I was until I smelled the cinnamon and nutmeg—despite what I knew of the pies and their sinister ingredients. Still, they looked so delicious. My mouth was watering.

I plunged my arm into one of the pies. They were completely cold now. I found no signs of liver, sinew, muscle, or bone. All I spotted were cherries. I penetrated another one, and broke apart the lattice of another. Cherries. Cherries. Cherries. Nothing but cherries. My father had made a dozen cherry pies. I sucked the filling from my arms and nibbled at the lattice. I did not bother spitting the pits out. Then I remembered the burlap sacks. They sat in the kitchen, just where my father had left them, but one of them was leaking now. A sticky red liquid saturated the bottom of the sack and spread out onto the floor.

Carefully, I peered into the bleeding sack. I discovered nothing but cherries.

The boys were in the other, curled up head to toe, as twin babes in their mother's womb. They were stone still, clad in their costumes. Still in one piece from what I could tell. Then the eye of the one boy spilled open, its dark center filling with light. It startled me, and I took a few steps back. But before long, I realized that aside from his eye, the boy and his brother were quite paralyzed.

I considered retiring to my room once more and locking myself inside. It is where I am most accustomed to being these last few months.

Instead, I found an ax beside the woodpile in my father's orchard. When it proved too cumbersome to heft, I rolled the sack of children across the kitchen floor instead. The boys did not make a noise as I kicked them into the dining room and to the edge of the hearth. They stayed quiet, even as I kicked them into the flames, which licked the burlap from their bodies and the flesh from their bones.

I remember a hole in the woods. I will remember more tomorrow. Pie is for breakfast. Cherry pie. Maybe then I will spit the pits out.

FOLLOW DARKNESS LIKE A DREAM
(A MIDSUMMER NIGHT'S DREAM)
ERIN KEATING

Up on the bald mountaintop, there was nothing but sky, and sky, and sky. Unfettered by trees, Hilda could see the distant spruce-blue peaks sprawling in every direction. Below her, the sloping hillside shone snow-white with blooming wineleaf and mountain bittercress. She came here when the town, with its dirt road and cabins and echoes of the mine far below, felt like it might suffocate her. Up here, the eager breeze carried her voice into the achingly blue sky. Some days, Hilda recited Goethe and Büchner in her parents' German. Other days, she sang imperfect Wagner and Mendelssohn. But today was Shakespeare.

"I know a bank where the wild thyme blows, where oxlips and the nodding violet grows, quite over-canopied with luscious woodbine, with sweet musk-roses and with eglantine." She let her voice ring out at the end of each line, not continuing until her echo had returned to her. The pale flowers tilted their faces toward her. The wind pressed closer. The mountains leaned in, listening.

By the time Hilda finished Oberon's monologue, shadows swelled over the waving grasses. A late evening fog, heavy and humid, rose from the valley below. On the brink of dusk, everything seemed possible: fairy glens, magic flowers, waking dreams. And yet, Hilda could not conceive of a single fantastical idea for a play of her own.

Midsummer was fast approaching, and Hilda had been tasked with writing a play for the annual festival. This was the first time Mr. Quince had broken tradition—he and the players had performed Shakespeare at each festival since he had arrived nearly a decade ago. He must have seen the resignation in Hilda's eyes; she was going to stay here, but he was kind enough to give her something of her own.

"What should I write?" she demanded of the bald.

"Something about young lovers perhaps?"

Hilda startled at the voice, her hand pressed to her racing heart. "Dietrich, how long have you been standing there?"

Dietrich ambled up the grassy path where clumps of purple heather had grown these past few summers, transplanted from the pocket of a homesick Scotsman. Her friend—no, her betrothed now—was so tall and lanky, Hilda marveled that he didn't sway in the breeze. When he stood beside her, she was merely half his height, even with his stooped shoulders. "They sent me to come get you." There was always that note of apology in his voice now, his eyes downcast.

Hilda pouted. "Please, a little longer. I haven't written a single word yet."

"Just a little longer. Perhaps it was such a lovely night, I stopped to smell the flowers." Dietrich smiled weakly and, not for the first time, Hilda wished that she could love him.

She could see it now—standing opposite him in her nicest dress with a penny in her shoe and cornflowers in her hair, her parents' doorstep littered with ceramic and stoneware smashed in celebration. Dietrich would look at her the way he had before their parents announced the engagement, like her eyes were lodestars and her voice a melody sweet as birdsong.

Dietrich would be a good husband. They would spend winters sitting by a hearth, Hilda reciting poetry and Dietrich listening with closed eyes. Hilda *wanted* to want him for everyone's sakes: their mothers', their fathers', for Dietrich's. It would be a fine life, Hilda reminded herself. Perfectly fine.

"Hmmm, young lovers," Hilda mused. Dietrich wanted something joyful, a comedy that ended in marriages upon marriages. But when Hilda imagined young lovers, she imagined the tragedies: *Tristan und Isolde, Orfeo ed Euridice, Romeo and Juliet*. She imagined spending the rest of her life in this town: the dirt road, the cabins, the rising ash.

All at once, the night seemed so close, the shadows wrapped around her shoulders.

Hilda pressed her feet hard into the rocky soil, her fists clenched. When she spoke, she almost didn't recognize her own voice. "See the shadows creep down the mountainside, swallowing the sweet wineleaf and the bittercress, gorging on the rocky outcrops, devouring the young man and woman standing alone. The shadows bring sleep and hateful fantasies."

The sun dipped below the mountaintop, haloing Hilda and Dietrich with its last light. Against the rising mist, their shadows towered, giants stretched across the clouds.

"*Brockengespenst!*" Hilda interrupted her new story for an old one. Tales her mother told of the mountains of her girlhood—of the clouds rising to the summit of the Brocken, of rainbows haloed over hikers, of human shadows grown to the size of giants. The Brocken Specter. "I never thought I'd see one!" Hilda grabbed Dietrich's arm, the way she would have when they were children, before everyone was so intent on their marriage.

"I don't see anything," Dietrich grumbled.

"Oh, perhaps it is because you are too tall. Bend down, look at my shadow!" The enormous shadow, crowned with a rainbow, did not waver.

Dietrich's stubbled cheeks drooped into a frown. "There is no need to tease. I gave you more time, and now you have written your first line. Let's go." He started back down the worn, wide trail.

Hilda waited a moment longer, marveling at the size of her shadow. It was all simply a trick of the light, she knew, that let someone so small cast a shadow so large. "Will I ever see you again?" Hilda asked. In all of her years, this was the first Brocken Specter she had seen. She wanted to stay with it, marveling until the illusion broke, until the sun set and could no longer illuminate the mist with its rainbows. But

Dietrich was calling her name, so she whispered her farewells and hurried after him.

Hilda's too-large shadow followed her home.

※

The next day, Hilda ran down the long dirt road toward the mountain path.

"Hilda, wait!" a breathless voice called.

Helen hurried down the road, a basket of fabric scraps bouncing against her hip. "I have questions about the costumes!" Everyone knew Helen was the finest seamstress in town, surpassing her own mother, with stitches fine as spider silk. She was the only person who could take scraps and turn them into a sorcerer's cape or a princess's gown.

"I haven't a play yet!" Hilda called to her friend.

"But—"

"Let me write it first, then we will discuss costumes. I promise!" Hilda quickened her short strides, until she stepped through the trees and the town vanished behind her.

She carried paper and ink in her bag, and the seed of an idea beginning to take root in her mind. There was something about the story she'd told Dietrich yesterday. The more she thought on it, the more she believed her words had conjured the Brocken Specter. She knew it was impossible for words to bend light and shadow, but still, she let herself dream.

When she broke through the tree line at the bald, the sky was shining desperately blue. It was midafternoon, and the sun beat down on Hilda's neck, casting short shadows.

"I have returned with a story," Hilda told the bald mountain.

The wineleaf and bittercress inched closer. The sky slunk down from its great height. The purple heather—not being from these parts—cautiously leaned nearer.

"We last left our lovers on this very hillside, the hungry shadow of midsummer stretching near. The shadow had fallen in love with the young woman and her golden voice, which could bring sunshine or clouds. It wanted to follow at her heels, wrap itself around her, keep her for itself."

Though no mist rose from the valley, though the sun was high, Hilda's shadow began to stretch long. It unfurled from her feet like a shimmering bolt of silk, too fine to be believed.

"*Brockengespenst*," Hilda breathed. Could it still be called a Brocken Specter if it wasn't a trick of the sun? But if it wasn't a trick of the sun, then what was it?

With every new line she spoke, the Brocken Specter grew darker, sharper, as though it were not a being of light, but of flesh.

"It longed to take the young woman to the realm of shadows, a place of darkness and dreams, where she would stay young and beautiful and nothing would ever change."

The Brocken Specter separated from Hilda's feet, hovering in midair. It extended over the edge of the hillside, until Hilda wondered if she was blotting out the light in the valley below. Perhaps they thought she was a passing cloud. Hilda wished she was—she could float past this too-quiet place, towards Washington or Philadelphia or New York, those legendary cities where people dressed in their finest gowns to watch performances under red velvet curtains and electric lights. But that was not to be her life, no matter how fervently she dreamed of it.

"In the realm of shadows, the spirits and the dark all applauded the young woman with her voice of gold." Hilda reached for her towering shadow.

The shadow did not move.

By the time Hilda realized the Brocken Specter was not her own shadow but a being of its own, it was too late. The darkness—cool and smooth—had taken hold of her wrist and pulled her down.

※

Hilda knew only muffled darkness and shades of gray. She could have sworn her eyes were open, but all she saw were shifting shapes made of mottled light. She reached out, trying to find something to steady herself with, but her hands were so heavy. Had they always been so heavy?

The space around her flickered, warm and haunting. Electric lights. Red velvet curtains. The squeak of polished boards beneath her feet. As she squinted into the light, she made out silhouettes in neat rows of seats, stretching back and back until they faded into the darkness. She was in a theater, on a real stage, not just the rickety carpentry and old linen sheets they erected every summer. The air hung heavy with perfume, the smell over-ripe like a dying garden.

And a voice from behind her, below her, all around her, said, "Speak."

Hilda began, "I know a place where the wild thyme blows."

But the voice whispered, the sound like the crackle of a flame and the rustle of sheets, "No. With your own words."

Hilda planted her feet squarely on the floor, and she spoke. She spoke of her bald mountain, of a sky so blue it would break your heart, of railroad lines leading away, away, away. With every word, she grew tired, her tongue lolling in her mouth, slurring her perfect diction.

The theater grew louder. She felt them, the silhouettes in the audience, turning real. Shadows becoming bodies with rustling skirts and lace fans straining against the summer heat. They shifted and murmured, and when Hilda finished her monologue, their applause sounded like an evening thunderstorm.

She nearly collapsed, the weight of her blood-red dress pulling her down. She hadn't always been wearing this dress, had she? She had never owned anything so fine in her life.

And the voice whispered, "Well done, my young one, my beautiful one, my golden voice."

"Who are you?" Hilda whispered, certain the audience would not hear her over their applause. Sleep pressed heavily against her. And yet, it was a gentle tiredness, the exhaustion of napping in sweet grass in the sunshine, the kind of weariness that promised pleasant dreams.

"Your dreams, of course," the voice said.

The red velvet curtain lowered, sound growing muted.

"Not yet," Hilda whispered. "Let me dream a little longer."

FOLLOW DARKNESS LIKE A DREAM

Hilda blinked herself awake.

"Good afternoon, sleeping beauty." Helen's teasing face hovered above her.

Soft fabric was pressed to her cheek, the bald and the low arching sun tilted sideways. Hilda's head rested in Helen's lap. Her scalp tingled, and she wondered if Helen had been finger-combing her hair while she rested.

"How long was I asleep?" Hilda asked, pushing herself up.

"I couldn't say. I thought you'd been up here an awfully long time and went looking for you. When I found you, you were curled up asleep."

Hilda held out her hands. They were no longer heavy. The dress she wore was a plain linen smock, not a crimson ball gown. It was a dream, of course. But what a marvelous dream. "I have the play, I just need to write it down." She rummaged for her paper and ink.

Helen sat quietly beside Hilda, her skirt hitched up to feel the waning sun on her long legs. Hilda snuck glances, marveling at the sun-pinked skin. Her best friend had always been beautiful, but recently that beauty made something hum within Hilda, like a violin string plucked so that it rang and rang.

When Hilda pressed her pen to the paper, the words flowed as steadily as if someone were whispering them in her ear. It spoke in the voice of her dream: candle flame and sleep-rumpled sheets.

Once the pages were finished, Hilda set them in Helen's lap. She rested her cheek against her friend's shoulder as she read, breathing in the smell of sweat and sweet grass.

Their shadows shifted, fading as the light grew dimmer, behaving exactly as shadows ought. What a strange dream that had been.

Helen turned over the last page, and her face fell. "Is that all?"

"*All?*" Hilda huffed.

"The young woman stays trapped in the realm of shadows forever? Her lover doesn't save her?"

"Oh, and how do you propose he saves her?"

"Well, she's asleep, isn't she? Perhaps he kisses her and she wakes."

Hilda pouted. "That's how all of the stories end."

"Something different then. A flower made of moonlight, something that chases the shadows away. He anoints her eyes with it, and lets her see truly."

Hilda had to admit it was not a terrible idea. She liked the spectacle of it, could almost see the glowing flower cupped in the young lover's hand. Its glow against her own face would be lovely—for she had already cast herself in the role of the young woman.

"You could make something like that?" Hilda asked.

Helen nodded without hesitation.

Hilda sighed. "Fine. Just for you, I will give you a romance instead of a tragedy."

"You truly are too kind," Helen teased.

Their faces were so close, the night so dim. Hilda wondered if she curled her fingers in Helen's thick auburn hair, could they pretend it was all a dream come morning?

But a distant creature howled. The pale hairs on Hilda's arms stood on end. "Come, we shouldn't be out here so late." She gathered up her papers.

But Helen sat very still, her eyes cast up towards the stars. "What were you dreaming about earlier?"

"How do you know I was dreaming?"

"You were talking in your sleep, going on about railroads and cities and leaving." Helen turned to hold Hilda's gaze. No wonder Hilda thought the sky would break her heart—it was the same shade as Helen's eyes. "Are you planning on leaving?"

Hilda looked down at the papers clutched against her chest. Her heart sank into her ribs, each beat willing her to *go, go, go*. But she had her parents who had given her everything. She had Dietrich who was so kind and so good. She could not leave. The shadows grew darker as they bled into the night.

"I was just…dreaming."

Helen rose, standing a full head above Hilda. Hilda always hated craning her neck to look up at Dietrich, but she would do it for Helen. She would twist herself into knots and bend over backwards if it meant looking into Helen's face.

"Well, when dreaming becomes planning, I'm coming with you. Do you understand?"

But there would be no planning, not now, not ever. No betrayed parents. No broken engagement. She would stay in this town, writing plays for the midsummer festival, daring to dream of a different life only when the night was at its darkest.

Hilda's words were lost, that golden voice dying on her tongue. Instead, she linked her arm with Helen's, heading back toward town.

The summer evenings were perfect for rehearsal, the light lasting long after the day's work was done. The air was midsummer sweet, before the overripe, rotting heat of late summer crept through the mountains. As Hilda read her lines, she marveled at the looks on everyone's faces, the concentration with which they practiced her work.

I made this, Hilda marveled. A week into rehearsal, she had nearly forgotten how she had fidgeted as Mr. Quince—her old schoolmaster—read her play, the sunlight off his spectacles making it impossible to guess where his eyes landed on the page. But, *finally,* he had tapped the edges of the pages and said, "Excellent work. Truly excellent work."

Folks from town came to watch them rehearse: Mr. Quince's doting wife, the young husband of the only other actress in the cast, and Dietrich sitting in the grass ramrod straight. And Helen, who joined them each day with a basket of scrap fabric in her lap, her needle darting faster than Hilda could see. Scraps of dark tulle and lace stitched together into a diaphanous cloak that would conceal the king of shadows.

And yet, Hilda wanted so much more. Hilda wanted her pages stitched and bound in linen. She wanted to project her words not into the purpling sky but into a hushed crowd. She wanted Helen's costumes to shimmer beneath electric lights.

This must be enough, Hilda reminded herself.

A shadow darkened the corner of Hilda's vision. But when she turned, there was only the line of tired trees. The longer she looked at them, the wearier she grew, until her legs felt like roots sinking into the dirt.

This must be enough.

※

Each evening, they rehearsed. Each night, she dreamed. She stood on that stage, light flickering against faces she couldn't make out. Night after night, they grew familiar until they looked like a mirror to her own. That voice whispered, all smoke and soft sheets, "Your dreams, your dreams." It sounded like it was smiling, just beside her ear.

Once, when the audience was applauding, she dreamed that Helen emerged from the wings, a bouquet of roses in her arms, her dress made of rippling shadows. Helen pressed her fingers to Hilda's cheek, and Hilda held her hand close.

That morning, she'd woken to find herself on the mountain, brambles snagged in her nightdress and her bare feet bleeding into the soft grass. In the gray dawn light, she wept for all of the things she could only have while she slept: a life on the stage, fine gowns, Helen.

When all her tears were spent, she laid very still, her body fixed to the ground by dread.

"I will never leave here," Hilda mourned to the pale shadows.

They seemed to answer, "We know." But it must have been the wind.

※

Rehearsals out on the hill had once felt so grand, the sky and the valley open all around, her voice as big as she liked. But after her dreams of that theater—of the crowd's adoration, of *Helen's* adoration—it all seemed so insignificant.

When they had a break at rehearsals, sometimes she snuck off into the trees to sleep, if only to plunge into the world of her dreams for a moment. When she woke, she could still feel the dream clinging to her, whispering beside her. Shadows danced at the edge of her vision, the air ringing with distant applause.

Helen walked home with her every evening, when the shadows were at their longest and the woods seemed at their nearest. Hilda swore she heard the swish of Helen's smoky dress across the stage. If Helen pressed her fingers to Hilda's cheek right then, would they be as warm and soft as they had been in her dreams?

On their last night of rehearsals, Helen stopped at the edge of the woods. The warm lights of nearby houses cast long shadows down the street. Hilda wanted to stand in that light, to watch her own shadow stretch long and terrible over the town that she would never leave. But Helen grabbed her sleeve.

"I think Nicholas might propose to me."

"Nicholas?" Hilda reeled. The actor playing the young hero. At each rehearsal, he read the lines Hilda had written with a suave sincerity that he'd perfected after years of playing the leading man. Hilda would have liked him more if he wasn't so terrifically full of himself. When had he ever shown an interest in Helen?

"Yes, and there's no need to sound so surprised. I'm not unmarriable," Helen huffed.

"But he's such an ass!"

"Perhaps I find him amusing."

"Do you—find him amusing?" Hilda pressed.

Helen hesitated. "He's as good a match as any. And now seems like a fine time to get married. He's interesting, sometimes."

She grabbed Helen's arm, heat radiating between their skin. "But do you love him?" Hilda demanded.

"Do you love Dietrich?" Her breath was so close, and so sweet.

The shadows seemed to press closer, whispering, "Your dreams, your dreams." The more Hilda resisted, the nearer they felt, until the shadows clung to her like a second skin. She closed her eyes, unable to look at Helen's parted, expectant mouth. "That's different. Dietrich is Dietrich. I don't—not like I—"

"Hilda! There you are!" Dietrich's voice carried through the woods. He stood at the very edge of the tree line, backlit by the lamps from town, his face obscured.

Helen tried to pull away, but Hilda held firm to her arm. "What will you say if Nicholas proposes?" she whispered.

Helen shrugged, her eyes cast to the ground. "I don't have a reason to say no."

Shadows danced at the edge of Hilda's vision, beckoning. Hilda's limbs seemed leaden. Helen would marry Nicholas. Hilda would marry Dietrich. This was to be their life—their too-small life.

"Go." Helen nudged Hilda away. "Dietrich is waiting."

Hilda's hand fell from Helen's arm, hanging limply at her side. Each step towards Dietrich felt as though she were trudging through mud. She couldn't even manage the strength to lift her head to look back: was Helen standing there, watching her go?

When she reached Dietrich, she slumped against him. He must have taken it as an affectionate embrace—did he not notice how heavy she had become?

He rambled cheerily, "Your folks are visiting with my parents. Our fathers have poured the beer and your mother has her violin and—"

This was the life she was to lead. Spending evenings with her parents and Dietrich, singing and drinking until the night sprawled into dawn. A fine life. A perfectly fine life.

So why did the very thought of it press Hilda deeper into the ground?

"I'm sorry, Dietrich, I can't." Hilda's words slurred with sleep. "I'm too tired."

※

That night, sprawled across her sheets, Hilda whispered, "Take me there."

The darkness listened, the shadows of her bureau and bed turning into dancing, winged creatures that carried dreams on their backs. They covered her like a blanket, settling in the crook of her elbow, tucking themselves under her chin.

They breathed out like a sigh, "Your dreams."

And then she was on that stage again.

She had entered the dream mid-song. Her own voice filled the theater with golden light. In the seats, the shadows danced. For the first time, Hilda saw them clearly, creatures of wings and horns and crowns of flowers. She felt so light there, like she could float to the ceiling, painted to look like the sky.

"My young one, my beautiful one, my golden voice," her shadow whispered.

Hilda turned from the audience and their delighted cries, facing upstage. Her shadow, as enormous as a Brocken Specter, towered up the back wall. It rippled in the electric lights, stretching away, then pressing close. It draped over the back of her neck, curving against her spine. It smelled like sweat and sweet grass, sounded like the rustle of Helen's skirts. Her shadow was everything she wanted; everything she could never have.

And she wanted so very much.

"You could stay here," her shadow whispered. "Stay and have everything you want."

On cue, Helen appeared from the wings. The crowd had hushed behind them, shadows dissolving into the plush seats. They were alone: Helen, draped in a smoky robe that fell off her shoulders; Hilda, draped in shadow and desperate want.

Helen closed the distance between them at a run, her robe fluttering open to reveal sun-pinked nakedness. Hilda fell into her, hands in hair, lips on neck, a whimper of pleasure.

"I want to stay with you," Hilda breathed into the delicate hollow of Helen's collarbone. "If this is a dream, don't let me wake."

Helen spoke with the voice of Hilda's shadow, "You have such delicious dreams."

⁂

"Hilda," a voice whispered. "Hilda."

It was familiar. Hilda floated towards that voice like she was floating toward the surface of a pond. Everything around her dark, whispering, but that voice rippled like light.

"Hilda."

It wasn't Helen's voice. It wasn't so warm Hilda melted at the sound of it. In fact, that voice was sharp, scared.

No.

Hilda woke sweat-slicked.

Late morning sun poured in through her window. Her legs were tangled in soaked sheets. Her mother sat beside her.

"My sweet one," she said in German. Whether her mother spoke with relief or chastisement, it was hard to tell. "You wouldn't wake."

Hilda blinked at her mother. Her graying hair was parted severely down the middle, her eyes rimmed with tired circles. That would be her face soon. How long would it take? Five years? Ten?

"Oh, there is no need for tears." Her mother wiped her face with the hem of her sleeve.

Hilda hadn't even realized she was crying. She had been in Helen's arms in a velvet darkness that smelled like a midsummer night. And now she was here.

"Leave me alone," Hilda hissed. She buried her face in her pillow, as though that would send her back to the world of dreams. "Please," Hilda begged of the shadows. But the light was unkind, too bright, too steady.

"Oh, come now. That is enough of that." Her mother sat on the edge of the bed. She folded Hilda against her chest, her cheek pressed to Hilda's forehead. "Tell me what is wrong. Are you unwell?"

I cannot bear to be awake, Hilda wanted to weep. But instead, she squeezed her eyes tighter, praying the darkness would come for her and give her everything she wanted.

"Ah, I know what it is. You are sad because after tomorrow the festival will be over. You'll have to wait a whole year for the next play. Oh, but what a year it will be, my sweet one. You will be married. You will have your own house. God willing, you will have your own child. See, there is nothing to cry over."

Each item in that litany of blessings twisted like a knife between Hilda's ribs. Her mother, and her father, and Dietrich, they would be so happy. They would smile, while Hilda cursed the sun for rising each morning.

She did not want a husband, a house, a child. She wanted to be free of this place, to take Helen by the hand and jump on a train and *go*. Perhaps people would tell their story one day, a young woman with a voice of gold and a young woman who stitched fairytales from fabric scraps, who ran away to a place big enough to hold them.

But Hilda searched her mother's eyes, which brimmed with tears now too. Her mother had taught her all about leaving. She had left behind a country, a language, a family. You left your home because you were starving. You left your home because whole villages burned across the horizon. You did not leave your home because you *wanted* to.

Hilda rubbed her eyes, trying to wipe away the last remnants of sleep, though it broke her heart to do so. Then she patted her mother's cheek. "Oh, *Mutti,* it will be a wonderful year, won't it," she said in her golden voice. That voice could fool anyone. Even her mother.

Even herself.

Midsummer's day began with a wedding—the midwife's son and a young woman who looked like she'd found a soft place to land. The whole town was drunk on blackberry gin by the time the pageant started. Twinkling paper lanterns hung around the stage—a hasty wooden construction by the carpenter who doubled as an actor. Helen had patched their old backdrop with big yellow stars stitched with golden thread so they caught the shimmering light.

Hilda peeked from behind the curtain: people were settling on blankets spread on the grass. The bride and groom shone with a loving blush. Dietrich sat in the back, a bouquet of daisies tied up with string in his hand. She wished she could be as good to him as he was to her.

Mr. Quince welcomed everyone to this year's midsummer pageant, congratulated the bride and groom, soliloquized in ways only Mr. Quince could soliloquize.

The whole scene felt eerily like Hilda's dreams, the shadows of the audience pulsing in the light, her own shadow too heavy and too close. If she closed her eyes now, would she simply drift off where she stood?

"What are you doing?" Nicholas hissed beside her. Nicholas—the one who was going to propose to Helen. His features seemed hidden in shadow, warped into something grotesque. But his voice was clear. "That's your cue." And he shoved her out from behind the curtain.

The performance began. Hilda took the stage in a dress of pale sky blue, the color of Helen's eyes. She spoke the words she had said all those weeks ago when she'd brought her shadow to life.

"See the shadows creep down the mountainside, swallowing the sweet wineleaf and the bittercress, gorging on the rocky outcrops, devouring the young man and woman standing alone. The shadows bring sleep and hateful fantasies."

It seemed wrong to speak of them that way. Not when the world they had shown her was so perfect. Not when they had given her everything she had ever wanted.

She felt the shadows moving around her. At first, she only sensed them out of the corner of her eye, inching closer when she looked away. But they grew bolder, dancing around the unseeing audience. Hilda played to them like she had every night, delighting in the way they flickered with joy.

When Mr. Quince wrapped his smoky cloak around her shoulders, she gave a half-convincing cry of distress. What she wouldn't give to be swallowed up by the shadows again and taken to the world of her dreams. Soon, soon, soon the play would be over, and Hilda could sleep. The candles they'd placed across the stage as footlights were burning fast, the scenes were moving quickly, and, *finally,* she was draped in Nicholas's arms, her eyes closed and limbs tangled in the shadowy cloak.

Nicholas spoke the words Hilda had written just for Helen, about a flower that bloomed from a drop of moonlight, whose nectar could chase away any dream, banish any shadow.

Weeks ago, a lifetime now, Helen had showed Hilda the flower she'd created. It was like a little piece of magic stitched at her fingertips, each petal sewn from a different piece of satin, shimmering in a prism of color. Along the petals, tiny starbursts were embroidered in silver thread, dotted with glass beads small as grains of sand.

She heard the audience gasp as Nicholas brandished the flower from his coat. It must have been stunning, the way the twinkling lights of the candles and lanterns caught in its shimmering petals.

Hilda would dream about that flower tonight. She would dream of laying Helen down in a field of moonflowers, their bodies beaming with light.

And yet, the shadows waited. Even as Hilda took her bows—once as an actress and once as the playwright—the shadows did not press past the edge of the stage. Oh, but she wanted them to. She wanted the shadows to snatch at her ankles and tear at her dress as the footlights guttered and died. She wanted them crazed. She wanted them to pull her down into their throng until she could never resurface.

Out in the audience, everyone she had ever known applauded her. It had been a lovely little show, they'd say. They'd eagerly wait for another one next year. They'd hug her and congratulate her on her betrothal, and she would see them again the next day, and the day after that, and the day after that. The people out there, they were like morning sunlight: steady and unwelcome.

Hilda did not want sunlight. She wanted only the moonflower's satin petals, only the night's sweet promises, only her dreams. She slipped back behind the curtains. And she ran.

Hilda didn't bother with the path. She tore into the woods, searching for the corners where light had never reached. She would find a bed of moss, a lullaby in the birdsong.

Hilda felt the shadows pressing in. They reached from the darkness, caressing her hair, whispering encouragements, "Your dreams, your dreams."

Each step grew heavier, her feet dragging as though her own body was holding her back.

Her shadow pressed close, wrapping its arms around her ribs like a lover. "Your dreams, your dreams," the shadow murmured.

Hilda fell into soft leaves, the forest floor sweet with the smell of rot. She would sleep here. She would sleep forever.

❧

Hilda was on the stage again. She was on the stage, and darkness spewed from her mouth, blanketing the whole theater in shadow.

Her song was a scream.

"What is this?" She strained against the cries that poured from her unbidden. She tasted blood in her mouth when she fought to make her words her own.

"Your dreams. Your want," her shadow said.

"These are not my—"

The song took over again. One low note of agony rang through the theater.

The stage and the lights and the velvet were gone, utter darkness in its place.

"I want to wake up." Helen choked, her mouth full of blood. The shadows in the audience laughed, wings rippling, horns gleaming. They screeched like circling carrion.

She swayed on her feet. How was she still standing? Everything was so heavy. Her head. Her arms. Her feet. The stage floor should have buckled underneath the weight of her.

"I want—" But the words warped on her tongue, jagged and metallic.

The shadows screamed for it, pressing up against the stage, hands pulling her down. The darkness could not be satisfied, no matter how she sang into it or screamed into it, it demanded more of her. It tore at her throat, trying to get at whatever was inside her.

Distantly, she thought, *I asked for this, didn't I?*

Hilda was cracking down the center, hungry claws leaving burning trails through her flesh.

"My dreams are not yours," she spat.

She thought that speaking it might make it so, the way she had conjured the Brocken Specter that evening on the bald and created shadows from nothing. But perhaps those shadows had always been there, and it was childish to think that because she named them, they answered to her.

The dark answered to no one.

"Your dreams," her shadow repeated as it gorged on her.

A dream, a dream, a dream, Hilda thought as she dissolved into the darkness. *Think but this and all is mended, that you have but slumbered here.* What were the rest of the words? She had known them once. She had proclaimed them to the mountains and the mountains had echoed them. *And we fairies that do run...following darkness like a dream.* Was that it? She was so tired, her limbs so heavy she was not sure if she had limbs anymore.

She would sleep. It was what she had wanted, wasn't it? To sleep away the rest of her life. Too-small, too-quiet life. *No more yielding but a dream.*

Then a shriek rent the darkness. A pale light poured in like a heartbreaking blue sky. The shadows recoiled from the light, from the gentle voice that came with it.

"I'm coming with you," the voice insisted, over and over.

The shadows' wings shrank, their horns thinned, until they were not shadows at all but ferns and mushrooms and broken branches littering the forest floor.

And even though Hilda did not believe there was any of herself left, she let the light wrap around her and press two kisses on her eyelids.

Hilda woke with Helen's lips hovering just above her skin. "There you are," Helen murmured as her eyes fluttered open.

They were in the forest, the air around them hushed and humid. "I told you a kiss would work," Helen whispered.

Hilda stretched her limbs. They moved freely, not weighed down by slumber. The shadows didn't cling to her the way they had those many weeks, sticky and warm, luring her to sleep. Her body was her own. Her thoughts strung together, one thought neatly after the other. She felt awake.

And yet—and yet—she still wanted.

Hilda was awake, and she wanted. She was so tired of wanting.

Hilda buried her face in the crook of Helen's neck. She pressed her mouth to the soft skin. Helen gasped, hugging her tighter to her chest.

"Does this mean—you're ready to leave?" Helen's lips brushed Hilda's forehead.

She thought of Dietrich. She thought of her parents and all they had taught her about leaving: leaving did not come from want, but from desperate need. If she stayed, she would sleepwalk through the rest of her life, wanting—no, *needing*—to be somewhere else. Her need, her want, her dreams would fester into shadow. It would devour her until nothing was left.

Hilda's teeth grazed Helen's earlobe, as she whispered, "Yes."

They stumbled down the path, tripping and tangling themselves up in each other. In the valley below, a train chugged in and out of the mining town, carrying iron and stooped workers.

Hilda and Helen would ride that train until they found a city of electric lights, a place that knew nothing of Brocken Specters or bittercress or mountain balds. There, the midsummer air would not be overripe with want. There, shadows would not hunger for dreams.

DISCOVER MORE

Thank you for taking the time to read *Violent Delights & Midsummer Dreams*. Reader reviews help small presses and indie authors thrive, and we appreciate your honest feedback. Please consider leaving us an honest review. We sincerely thank you for your continued support.

Other Anthologies by Quill & Crow

Eros & Thanatos: An Anthology of Death & Desire

Ravens & Roses: A Women's Gothic Anthology

Grimm & Dread: A Crow's Twist on Classic Tales

AUTHOR BIOGRAPHIES

Melissa Brinks (she/her) is a writer, editor, critic, podcaster, and snack connoisseur. Her books, The Compendium of Magical Beasts and The Little Book of Video Games, are available now from Running Press. Find her online at melissabrinks.com.

Sabrina Howard (she/her) writes from southwest Idaho with an endless supply of tea and a cat who's afraid of YouTube ads. Her work has previously appeared in the Grimm & Dread anthology from Quill & Crow Publishing House and the Houses of Usher anthology from Love Letters to Poe.

Erin Keating (she/her) earned her B.A. in creative writing and literature at Roanoke College and her M.A. in history at Drew University, mostly so she could continue to surround herself with old books. She currently works as a grant writer at an arts education nonprofit. When she isn't reading or writing, she is rock climbing, playing video games, or learning bass guitar. Her fiction has appeared in Quill & Crow Publishing House's *Bleak Midwinter Vol. II: Solstice Light,* Cosmic Horror Monthly's *Aseptic and Faintly Sadistic,* and Hungry Shadow Press's *It Was All a Dream* anthologies.

LK Kitney (they/them) lives in Orkney, Scotland, surrounded by tempestuous waters, wild open skies, and very few trees. Steeped in folklore, mythology and the weird from a young age, they have always been drawn to the gothic and the dark and have no plans to find their way out just yet. When not writing about problematic magic, they can be found beach-combing, crafting, or playing TTRPGs. First published in 2018 by Schreyer Ink Publishing, they also have a novella: *The Lies We Tell Ourselves,* now available from Luna Press Publishing.

Amelia Mangan (she/her) is an author currently living in Sydney, Australia. Her stories have been featured in a number of publications, including *The Best Horror of the Year Volume 11* (ed. Ellen Datlow), *The Book Smugglers* website (eds. Ana Grilo and Thea James), and *Bleak Midwinter Volume I: The Darkest Night* (eds. Cassandra L. Thompson and Damon Barret Roe). Her first novel, *Release,* was published by Nightscape Press in 2015.

Cedrick May (he/him) lives in the Dallas/Fort Worth area where he teaches African American literature and screenwriting at The University of Texas at Arlington. Cedrick has stories published or forthcoming in *Aphelion, Bourbon Penn, Coffin Bell, Dark Horses Magazine,* and *Road Kill: Texas Horror by Texas Writers, Volume 7.*

Mathew L Reyes (he/him) is a copy editor and writer of dark fantasy and horror based in Minneapolis. When he's not working as an editing gremlin, he's jogging, writing, and killing his darlings at the advice of his critique group. His works have appeared/are forthcoming in the NoSleep podcast, Bards & Sages Quarterly, the *Unspeakable Horror 3* anthology, and more.

Emma Selle (she/her) has loved stories since she can remember. She's always telling them, whether with pen and ink or with passionate arm-waving at a volume just slightly too loud. She especially loves Shakespeare, largely due to the influence of her mother. Currently, Emma writes like mad in between pursuing her undergraduate degree in Theatre & Business Administration. She is from Washington, the most beautiful state. She maintains a blog, *A Dose Of Ginger: A Storyteller's Collection of Stories to Tell,* where you can keep up with all of her exploits, authorly and otherwise.

William Steffen (he/him) is an assistant professor of English at American International College in Springfield, MA, where he teaches courses on Shakespeare, feminist horror films, cannibals in literature, and creative writing. His academic work on the early modern English stage has been featured in the *Journal for Early Modern Cultural Studies* and in *Renaissance Drama*. His first academic book, *Anthropocene Theater and the Shakespearean Stage* was published earlier this year with Oxford University Press. He lives in Holyoke, MA with his wife and two children.

TRIGGER WARNING INDEX

Child abuse, endangerment, or death
Othello—An American Tragedy (implied CSA)

Death
All except *Follow Darkness Like a Dream*

Decapitation and/or dismemberment
Lend Me Thy Hand
Such Sweet Uncleanness

Domestic and/or emotional abuse
Lend Me Thy Hand
Othello—An American Tragedy
The Winds Did Sing

Graphic violence, gore, or murder
A Document in Madness
Lend Me Thy Hand
The Marriage of Beatrice Messina
Othello—An American Tragedy
Such Sweet Uncleanness
To Make the Devil's Blood Run Cold
We, Unhappy
The Winds Did Sing

Hauntings
The Marriage of Beatrice Messina

Racism and/or slavery
Othello—An American Tragedy

Sexual harassment or abuse
A Document in Madness

Suicide or suicidal ideation
The Marriage of Beatrice Messina
To Make the Devil's Blood Run Cold

Transphobia and/or detransition
The Winds Did Sing

Zombies, walking dead, reanimated corpse, or resurrection
A Document in Madness

Made in the USA
Columbia, SC
16 June 2023

a6e30385-a036-4e47-bce6-42ae97c75ad4R01